INTO THE HURRICANE

Neil Connelly

ARTHUR A. LEVINE BOOKS
An Imprint of Scholastic Inc.

Library of Congress Control Number: 2017009604
ISBN 978-0-545-85381-1

10 9 8 7 6 5 4 3 2 1   17 18 19 20 21
Printed in the U.S.A.   110

First edition, July 2017
Book design by Mary Claire Cruz

For Beth,
again and always,
with a nod to the many storms
we've weathered together

Prologue

MAXINE FONTENOT CONSIDERS THE FRAMED SIGN HUNG ON the wall in the main office of the Clayborne Funeral Parlor. WE HONOR THE DEAD BY SERVING THE LIVING. Just above the sign, there's an imperfection in the wall, a tiny raised patch where some lazy painter spackled an old nail hole but didn't sand it down. Max runs a finger over the shoddy work. The fact is, she's bothered by just about everything about this place—the cheesy harp music drifting down from ceiling speakers, the tacky carpet, and most of all the sterile smell, which reminds her of the hospital room over at Wayne Osteopathic.

Max turns to the funeral home director, a pudgy man sitting awkwardly behind his oversized mahogany desk. She can tell that she makes him uncomfortable, the way he keeps trying not to gawk at the metal stud popping from each nostril or her spiky green hair. She cocks her head at the sign. "So what's that supposed to mean?"

The director clears his throat. "It means mourning is a process. The dead are gone to us. In truth, we can do little for them. Our real obligation lies with those left behind to grieve. The, uh, the survivors."

"Sounds like a load of crap to me," Max says. "But I guess the dead aren't writing you any checks, right?" She walks to the chair across from Clayborne and drops into it, then slides one long leg over the other. Thin slits rip across her black jeans, exposing pale skin.

Clayborne sticks two fingers inside his shirt collar and tugs it away from his neck. "As I thought I'd made clear when you called, this isn't my affair. It's a matter for the family to discuss. Really, Ms. Fontenot, you need to talk to your mother."

"You don't say the last *t*," Max snaps. Everybody in Jersey makes this mistake. "It's *Font-a-no*. As for my mom, I haven't seen her in ten years." Her mother ran off to Canada with a musician she met in New York. She left no note, never even said good-bye. One morning she was simply gone. "That lady out there with the black veil just happened to marry my dad. I've talked to her about all I need to." Max thinks of the new dress, black and sleek, that Angie bought her for today. Right now, it's crumpled on the floor in a basement bedroom at the Gonzalezes'.

Max leans forward. "Look, I was there at the end. Only me and nobody else. I'm the one who heard my dad's dying wish." This is a lie, but it's a lie she hopes might serve her purpose. Max allows a few tears to slip from her eyes, smearing her black mascara. "You're so eager to serve the living?" she continues. "Let me have that can."

Clayborne gulps and blinks. With some effort, he rises

and shuffles around the desk, past a window where an air conditioner struggles. Through the window next to it, Max sees cars sliding by in the parking lot. Clayborne crosses behind her, and the double doors to his office squeak when he shuts them. As he returns to his chair, he offers her a flowery box of tissues, which she waves away.

"We call it an urn, Ms. Fontenot," Clayborne says, now pronouncing her name correctly. "I know this is a most difficult time for you and your family. The loss of a loved one is always accompanied by great pain and confusion. This isn't a day for hasty decisions you may regret later."

Max stands up, but Clayborne raises a silencing hand. "Allow me to finish, please. Your mother—pardon me, stepmother—has been named executrix of the estate. I can't possibly release the remains to you without her consent, and her intentions on that matter are unequivocally clear. Also, if I might add a personal observation, she seems to have other matters complicating her situation."

Max ignores this last line and decides to double down on her lie. "But this isn't what he wanted."

From his inside jacket pocket, Clayborne tugs an immaculate white handkerchief and dabs at his forehead. "We'll start shortly. Then, after the service, we'll bring your father's remains to his final resting place. It's quite lovely and not far from your church."

"Not my church," Max says under her breath. This was another new element Angie brought into her father's life, another change that cut her out.

"Be that as it may," Clayborne tells her, "all these things, they've been arranged, you see. Whatever the source of this dispute, I have no place in it. Please. You're placing me in a horribly awkward position."

Max drops back into the cushions of the large chair. "Well, hell, I wouldn't want you to feel awkward."

Clayborne bristles. "We're talking about professional codes of conduct. Legal obligations."

"But me and my dad," Max says, "we had a deal." Her mind slides to a distant past, pure and true: the drone of the highway, the crappy fast food and the cheap hotel rooms they stayed in on that long road trip to Louisiana, where her father was raised. In the wake of her mother's betrayal, they'd retreated there for nearly two weeks, trying to salvage what they could from the wreckage of their lives, making promises they swore they'd always keep. *Just us.*

Clayborne doesn't respond, just tucks the handkerchief away. They sit in silence for a time. He folds his meaty fingers together and holds them on the desk. Finally, Max decides it's time for Plan B. She says, "Okay. Okay. I get it. I'm sorry I yelled before. I know this is your job, and you're doing what you think is right."

Clayborne's tense expression eases, and he nods.

"But before we go out there and get on with things, could I have a minute alone with him? Not out there with all those people but just here, privately?"

The director studies her face for a moment. "It's highly

irregular, but I don't see the harm. I'm happy to do what I can to help those in mourning." Quietly, he exits the room.

Alone, Max remembers the best memory of all from that trip south, she and her dad alone at that strange lighthouse, the wide sky above them, the gulf spreading out before them like glass, his arms around her. How special she felt then. Now she glances at her wrist and the broken Hello Kitty watch, something she swiped from the Goodwill where she works part-time. Roaming the aisles, she examines the items people discard, the winter coats and toys and books that once were prized. Every now and then, Max tucks an item into her pocket — a pink wallet, a heart-shaped pendant — just because she can't bear to leave it alone on the shelf, unwanted.

When Clayborne returns, he's holding what looks to Max like a small silver trophy, the kind her basketball team won in junior high a few years back, coached by her dad. With great reverence, Clayborne sets the urn on his desk. Max understands what's inside the central chamber, but still, she grips for the lid. Clayborne raises a hand and says, "At this point, it's best to leave the urn sealed. But your father, he is in there."

She says, "Okay, then. Could I be alone with him like we talked about?" For effect, she sniffles and plucks a tissue from the box.

"Certainly," Clayborne says. He leaves again, closing the double doors.

At the instant the latch clicks, Max drops her tissue, grabs the urn by a silver handle, and heads for the window. In her pocket are the keys to her dad's Jeep, where she's already stashed the knapsack she stuffed earlier at the Gonzalezes'.

The window next to the dying air conditioner slides up easily. Outside, the August air is like a hot breath. Max wonders for an instant what Clayborne will do when he returns and finds his office empty. But then the stray thought is gone, and so too is Max, heading south, carrying her father in one hand, determined to keep her lighthouse promise.

Chapter One

DOWN HERE IN THE SHACKS, WE DON'T BURY OUR DEAD. WE can't. Dig too deep and you hit water. Don't dig deep enough, and the earth'll reject that coffin, spit it out with the first good rain. So our coffins need to sit on top of the ground, each encased in its own concrete box. Left like this, some say the dead can't really rest in peace, which is one reason folks figure Louisiana's got so many ghost stories. Every parish has a haunted plantation house with slave souls on the prowl, plus there's pirates still searching for lost treasure along our coast, ancient Acadian settlers wandering our swamps, even original natives like the Coushatta, the Choctaw, or the Chitimacha, all floating free between the living and the dead. Out here on Shackles Island, there's a dozen good ghost tales, even enough to draw some whacked-out tourists across the iron bridge now and again. But there's one spirit nobody comes looking for, one that haunts me and me alone, and that's my big sister, Celeste. She's been dead going on six years, but from time to time, she visits me still.

Even right now in this dusty workshop garage, the place

where I probably feel safest and most at home, I can tell she's nearby, watching. I just came out to get some nails—I've been boarding windows for an hour—but my projects distracted me. Looks like I'll never get a chance to repair Mr. Harry's weed trimmer, or Big Ned's chain saw. Without her TV/VCR, Ms. June won't be able to watch her old home movies. I clear some space off my worktable and get everything up off the ground, to at least give the machines a fighting chance when the waters come.

Of all the jobs I won't finish, the one that gets me most is Dr. Wood's antique brass clock. It kept perfect time for decades so long as he wound it regular, and then it just gave out. Over the summer, I've spent hours studying the clock's mechanical guts. And now, once again, I cradle it in two hands. The brass is cool to the touch, and the white face, circled by Roman numerals, has yellowed some with age. But the best part's inside. I set it facedown and unscrew the back plate, exposing the miraculous gears. Here now is the central ratchet wheel, the delicate cogs and anchors, the tiny coiled springs. I've removed each piece, inspected it, replaced it. Everything is how it ought to be. The clock just doesn't work.

Oh, give it up, Eli.

The voice sounds only in my head, but I turn. Celeste is sitting on the motorcycle I resurrected from the salvage yard in Hackberry last year, an ancient Ducati nobody thought I could make run again. Same as always, she's dressed in a plain white T-shirt and cutoff blue jeans, like she was the last time I saw her alive. Only her blue jeans aren't blue at all but gray, the same way her strawberry-blond hair is just sort of soft white. She looks like a life-sized charcoal sketch, not the cruddy ones I draw but like a Leonardo da Vinci sketch—a perfect copy, right down to the almond-shaped eyes. Right now, she squints at me with that look of disappointment I know so well.

Quit wasting your time.

In real life, Celeste was a gentle spirit. She was a bit fragile and prone to crying, but she read to me at night from her history books, taught me to fight back against the kids who picked on me for being short and skinny, took me on nature hikes where we'd wander the woods or scan the beach for perfect seashells. She was a good big sister. As a ghost, she's mostly a jerk. Maybe death does that to you.

Especially an ugly death.

I know better than to ask her forgiveness. Celeste never answers me when I try to talk to her. So I reach for the nails I came in here for in the first place, grab my hammer, and brush past her, out onto the hard dirt of our yard. The air feels tense and charged, and again I sense what's coming, a hurricane that shares my sister's name. As soon as I saw the list for this year's storms, there she was, right behind Hurricane Arturo, which fizzled out, and Hurricane Bertrand, which raged a while and threatened the Georgia coast before spinning back into the Atlantic. But Hurricane Celeste, she's not screwing around.

I climb the wooden stairs onto the porch and approach the final piece of plywood. All the other windows are boarded up good. I lift the last one into place and focus on pounding each nail into place. Each bang pops like a gunshot. When I finish, everything is silent.

Inside the house, the phone rings. I hustle into a living room with all the lights off and the windows completely darkened. It feels like a tomb. Guided by the ringing and the dull green glow of the handset, I get to the phone by the fifth ring, but when I see the Galveston number of my aunt's house, I don't reach for the receiver. In the blackness, I wait for the phone to stop, then imagine my mom talking. Soon enough, the red message light gets to blinking.

The wind picks up, whistling high through the tight spaces between the plywood boards and the windows. The sound is sharp and piercing, like a red-winged blackbird's cry. I feel for the coffee table, set down the hammer, and grope around for the remote control. Moments later, the Weather Channel flashes to life, making the walls of the living room glow blue. They're showing aerial footage of when Hurricane Celeste smashed through the southern tip of Florida a few days back, leveling half a county. Entire neighborhoods were reduced to splintered timber, as if a giant had taken a club to the mobile homes and mansions. Seventy-five are dead in her wake. The image shifts to a satellite shot, a surging mass of swirling clouds, spinning like a buzz saw toward the exposed Louisiana coast.

The TV cuts back to the control room, where there's a whole gang of giddy meteorologists falling over one another with dire predictions, grinning with delight at doom and disaster. "Storm of the new century," they say. "Destruction on a massive scale!" They make it sound like we're facing the end of the world.

And, hey, that'd be okay by me.

I return to the phone, punch the button. My mom's recorded voice says, "Eli, I'm praying this means you're not there, that you're already on the road. You were supposed to call before you left. I wish you'd called. This thing is only getting worse—it's coming much quicker than they said—and the highways are crazy. If for some reason you're hearing this, sweet Jesus, get out of there. But, please, just call me first and let me know you're okay."

I feel about a billion miles from okay, but my mom doesn't want to hear that. Far as I know, everybody in the Shacks has packed up and fled north to higher ground. My parents bailed two whole days ago, steering their boat, the *Celestial Girl*, west along the coast down past the Sabine Pass. I guess they weren't going to lose her twice.

On the TV, they switch to footage of I-10, packed bumper to bumper in both directions. Folks don't know if they should head west for Houston or east to Baton Rouge. As for me, I have no impulse to run. I kind of like the idea of being alone on the island. For reasons I don't fully understand and can't explain, I just don't feel like that storm's the biggest threat in my world. One thing I've figured out in the six years since Celeste's death: It's damn near impossible to evacuate from yourself.

I'm surprised to see them cut to a satellite image of the Shacks. From high above, the east end and the west, each about three miles long, really do seem separate. Fact of the matter is it's all one island, shaped sort of like a figure eight or an hourglass. The name came from pirates who looked at the two linked masses on the maps and saw shackles.

A blond commentator, perky and smiling, says, "Residents of the region are complying with the governor's mandatory evacuation order."

I guess that makes it official. I'm the sole living citizen left on Shackles Island. I listen for Celeste and don't hear her, but I'm sure she hasn't gone far. For years I told nobody about my sister's ghost, how from time to time she'd show up—at my eighth-grade graduation, at my fourteenth birthday party. But the pressure of her presence built up inside me till my secret slipped out a couple summers ago. Late one night down on Holly Beach, I built a little driftwood fire under the stars, and this girl Sandra huddled inside my arm and everything felt right and good. She turned her face to mine, and I realized this would be it, my first kiss, and I closed my eyes and moved my lips to hers. That's when I heard *Spare me!*

I yanked my head back and saw Celeste, etched in black and white, shaking her head. Sandra blinked for a few seconds, then asked me what was wrong.

"It's Celeste," I answered without thinking. "Sometimes I see her."

Sandra pulled back and looked at me. "But Celeste is dead." Everybody on the island knows about the lighthouse.

I pointed at my sister and said, "Tell her that."

After Sandra glanced over her shoulder and saw nothing, she stood up and dusted the sand from her legs. She said, "Eli, you're a sweet guy and all, really. But you need some way serious help. Something ain't right in you."

Sandra's words landed hard, mostly because I'd come to that same conclusion. I guess she held her tongue for as long as she could, but by Halloween, kids at school were asking me if I'd seen any ghosts. When my parents heard the rumor, the two of them nearly bust. They'd each sort of fallen apart after Celeste's death, and they drove me over to Father Arceneaux at St. Jude's for what turned out to be an intervention, one with plenty of praying and crying. The charcoaled ghost of Celeste watched, giggling at my ordeal from the back pew. After Father Arceneaux couldn't exorcise her spirit, my mom drove me up to Lake Charles every Friday afternoon for a few months, where I sat in a room that smelled like mint and "talked it out" with a doctor who specialized in head cases. Dr. Jody asked lots of questions about how I felt, and I kept mostly quiet. One afternoon she casually asked, "Eli, have you ever thought about hurting yourself?"

Since that night with Sandra on the beach, I'd had a few weird notions, sure. In art class when I was cutting with an X-Acto knife, I found myself contemplating the blade's tip and the blue pathways of the veins on my wrist. And when we passed over the I-10 bridge in Lake Charles, tall enough for ships to pass beneath, I imagined what it'd be like to feel the wind, have the water rush up to meet me. But in Dr. Jody's office, I forced a smile and said, "Why would I do that?"

This pleased her, and I finally got a clue. For all involved, it was best if I got "cured." So I figured out the words everybody wanted me to say and swore my visions had stopped. I told them Celeste had left me in peace. When I got home from that last session, she was in the tire swing hanging from the live oak. She grinned my way and winked. *Our little secret.*

I know she's nearby now. Just like I know this hurricane with her name is no coincidence. I can feel my sister giving me a chance to make things right. Me and her, we got a plan, and she's not about to let me back out.

I'm thinking this very thought when there's a loud knocking on the front door—three angry bangs. After the jolt to my heart, I recover quick and tap down the volume on the TV, then lift the hammer from the coffee table. I slide up alongside the door, settle my back against the wall, and listen.

"Eli!" a voice yells. "Something about the term 'mandatory evacuation' fail to penetrate that thickened skull?"

I open the door and greet Sheriff Trouille. His white moustache needs a trim, and his face is stubbled with five o'clock shadow. I say, "I told my mom I'd finish boarding up the house. I thought I was the last one on the island. Just packing my things." As evidence, I show him my hammer.

"Uh-huh," Trouille says. "Well, your mother got through to me at the station and raised all kinds of hell, insisting I come check on you. Imagine my surprise to actually find you here. Son, that storm is a Category Five. You know what that means?"

"It means it's big. I know that."

"Well, there ain't no six on the scale, boy, so yeah, it's

about big as they come. When Hurricane Audrey hit back in the fifties, the water stretched near thirty miles up to the airport. By morning, I expect where we're standing now will officially be part of the Gulf of Mexico. So unless you're planning on growing gills or that motorcycle's got a submarine mode, it's time to get your butt on it and head north."

I look around the yard, where his squad car sits, and try to imagine the ocean in this far. Trouille says, "The governor has ordered we raise the iron bridge by five o'clock, way ahead of landfall. He's worried some TV crews or out-of-town loonies might try to get on the island in search of a front-row seat. I assured him all our local loonies would be long gone by then."

I ask, "So everybody else is gone?"

Trouille frowns. "Except the ones I can't convince. Yesterday I drove out to the Odenkirk place and visited Mother Evangeline, what with her special circumstances and all, but I couldn't talk sense into her. Seems she sees God's hand in this, like everything. And Sweeney's got it in his head that it's his patriotic duty to protect this land—from what, I'm not entirely sure. Anyway, he's hunkering down at that glorified tree house of his. The folks at FEMA told me to instruct anyone who insists on staying to write their Social Security number down their forearm with a permanent marker."

"Say what now?"

"Like with a Sharpie. To make it easy to identify the body later. Real cheery, those FEMA people."

"That's a scare tactic," I say. "Just trying to freak folks out."

Trouille holds my eyes. "Well, it'd work on me, I'm telling you. I know you've had some problems, son, but it's time to screw your head on straight. You hearing me?"

"Yeah," I tell him. "Yes, sir."

"Good, 'cause I don't give a damn about your personal rights. Your momma, she's endured enough. Once we're done at the station, I'm swinging back out this way. If you're still here, I'll arrest you for the fun of it and transport your scrawny butt over that bridge in handcuffs. Don't test me, son."

In the last nine months, Trouille's had me in handcuffs twice, so I know he's not bluffing. Behind closed doors, once I've calmed down, he's always talked to me with kindness. He convinced the wronged parties—each of whom deserved the whooping I gave them—not to press charges, probably telling them all kinds of personal details I'd rather he not share. At Celeste's funeral mass at St. Jude's, as Father Arceneaux spoke of God's mysterious ways, I can remember Trouille in uniform, his face all teary, standing over her coffin. I helped carry it out to the hearse, but when they brought it up to the cemetery in Hackberry, I refused to go.

"I won't be here," I tell him. "I promise."

He stares into my eyes, searching for the truth. "Be sure you're not."

I head over to the garage and Trouille walks beside me. When I reach up to close the door, he glances into my workshop and his eyes go wide. He's looking at the second bay, where Celeste's red pickup rises up like some dusty tombstone.

The front grille is still smashed in. The windshield is still shattered. "Is that the—?" He knows better than to finish the question. Instead, he just runs a hand across his moustache and states the obvious. "They kept it all this time?" he asks. "Never had it repaired?"

I pull the door down. "Some things aren't meant to be fixed."

Trouille sighs before turning to his squad car. He takes a few steps, then stops. Without facing me, he says, "She'd want you to be safe. You know that, yeah?"

By his somber tone, I know he's not talking about my mother. I look around for Celeste. The yard is empty, and there's no one on the porch. "It's not for you to say what my sister'd want."

The sheriff hesitates for a moment, then opens his door. "Stay safe, son." He gets behind the wheel, backs up into a K-turn, and steers away. I stand there, under the graying sky, watching him go.

Inside the house, I head for Celeste's bedroom. Dad wanted to take all her stuff to the Salvation Army, but Mom refused to touch anything, so her room is the same today as it was six years ago. Open one of Celeste's dresser drawers and you'll find neatly folded clothes, waiting for her return. Her maps of Africa and posters of ziggurats and European castles are still tacked to the walls, and her bookcase is crammed with sideways books—not kissy-kissy romance crap, but history, philosophy, world religion. On her desk sits a sphinx figurine. Next to it a stone Buddha meditates.

From under her pillow, I pull my latest sketchbook and slide up onto the bed. Among my earliest memories is picking busted crayons from a shoebox with Celeste, the two of us working on a coloring book. All through grade school, I doodled in the margins and even made my own comic strips. These days, I'm not half bad with a decent charcoal pen, and some of my drawings don't suck. As I flip through the over-sized pages, I pause on one sketch where I tried to catch the view out the window here, looking over the stretch of grassy wetland. Behind that one, there's a dozen attempts at Celeste's smiling face. I always struggle with the unique shape of her eyes, which used to make folks ask her if she had an ancestor from Asia. Even beyond the shape, her eyes were special. They used to shine with such love, such joy and hope. I can never capture that emotion on the page.

Fact is, the first time she came back to me, I was drawing. I was sitting right here on her bed, erasing and re-sketching till the page was wearing thin, and she appeared, a master-piece fully drawn. She looked at my attempt and said what I was thinking. *That really stinks. You'll never get it right.*

When Mom drove me up to the University of Louisiana at Lafayette for freshman orientation last month, I wasn't all that interested in the dorms or the gym or the big rooms where I'll supposedly take classes toward my degree in business marketing (handpicked by Dad). Mostly I'd agreed to go because my parents will be happier without me moping around here day in and out. But when I was figuring out my schedule, this advisor guy showed me a list of electives, and my eyes fell on Basics of Drawing. There was one seat left.

As we were leaving campus, I imagined my future self, leaning back onto the base of a magnolia tree just ahead, sketchbook on my lap, far away from Shackles Island. At college, nobody would know anything about me and my past. Something felt like it was rising inside me, a shining thing, and that's when Celeste stepped out from behind the tree, cast in black and white. *I didn't get to go to college,* she said in my mind. *Why should you?*

On the car ride home from Lafayette, Mom asked me why I didn't seem excited anymore. I told her my stomach was bugging me, and she left it at that.

For a few days, I tried to brush away what had happened on campus, but my brain kept dragging me back. It was the first time in a while Celeste had shown up, maybe months, but her appearance in that quad made it clear she'd be there when I went to school. In the classroom when my professors lectured, in the library when I was studying, at the dorm or cafeteria or soccer field when I was trying to make new friends. I knew then that Celeste would shadow me for the rest of my days. So not long after that college trip, when Dad's regional manager flew in from Dallas and Mom asked me to come along to a fancy crawfish dinner over at DI's, I begged out and stayed home. I sat at Celeste's desk and wrote a letter to Mom, apologizing for how I'd failed her and the fights I'd gotten into, sorry for being such a poor excuse for a son. I wasn't sure when

I'd use it, but I kept the note, just for security, folded up neat in the back of this sketchbook. I'd pull it out every now and then, in private, puzzling over how to do the thing I knew had to be done. Imagine my surprise and delight when I first heard word of this hurricane. It was a golden opportunity, a disaster sent to save me.

It's not that I've ever wanted to be dead. I don't want to be dead. I'm just sick of being alive like this.

So get on with it, I hear in my head. Celeste is suddenly sitting at her desk next to me. *What you waiting on?*

She's got a point. I'd figured on spending the afternoon here, heading out in the evening as the storm came on, but Trouille has forced my hand. I can't risk being here if the sheriff comes back. After a quick shower, I slip on my cargo pants and a gray T-shirt, my good hiking boots. From under my bed, I tug out my backpack. I scoop up the last few treasures from my beachcombing days with Celeste—the shells and the feather, the piece of smoothed glass. When I'd discover some special object on our hikes and bring it to here, she always said the same thing: *Attaboy.* Lord, I miss hearing her say that.

Out of habit, I grab two water bottles and a couple apples from the fridge, a handful of granola bars from the pantry. Recalling how dark it can get inside the lighthouse, I swipe Dad's good flashlight from the laundry room.

I cross our yard and slip inside the workshop, where I get the bolt cutters and shove them in my backpack too. One last time, I pull down the garage door and lock it up.

On the horizon's edge, Hurricane Celeste has made the sky gray. The rain still hasn't started, but you can feel it, hanging damp in the late-morning air. Only after I climb on my motorcycle do I realize I've forgotten my helmet in the house, but I don't guess I'll be needing it all that much. I slide in the key, lean up on one leg, and kick-start the engine. Then I cruise down the dirt driveway to Infinity Road.

At the T-shaped crossroads, I pause and drop a foot to steady myself. Turning right will lead me past the water tower and marina, toward town. I'd pass the iron bridge that leads over the intercostal and north. Up there, I could weave through traffic, be in my cousin Harvey's place in DeQuincy in a couple hours, dry and safe.

But when I glance in the opposite direction, away from town and the iron bridge, I see Celeste. Her charcoal ghost walks away from me down the shoulder of the road like some wandering hitchhiker. I know she wants me to follow.

I crank the handlebars hard left and give the engine gas. Dirt and grit kick up as the back wheel fishtails, and I swing out onto Infinity Road. My hair blows back as I race west past my ghostly sister, on toward the thin strip of land that connects the two halves of the island. I know she'll accompany me, that her haunting will go on. And I nearly smile at the thought of where I find myself headed—the last lighthouse in Louisiana, where Celeste and me will face the end together.

Chapter Two

SHACKLES ISLAND HAS THIS LONG TRADITION OF BEING A home for castaways and misfits. If you listen to legend, the infamous pirate Jean Laffite buried treasure here, and the outlaw Leather Britches had a hideout in the marshy forests. To help ships avoid the shallows around the island and guide them into the Sabine Pass, they put up a lighthouse in 1846. Prisoners from the Mexican-American War built it—forced labor in the Louisiana humidity. A bunch died, and some of their troubled souls still haunt the marshlands. That's the kind of crap that gets shoveled to the tourists. For a hundred years, the lighthouse beamed, but over time it was shut down and abandoned, all but written off. Maybe that's one more reason why I'm drawn to it.

White as bone, steady and constant, she rises up to a height of two hundred feet. Even from a couple miles away, doing seventy miles an hour straight down the center line of Infinity Road, I can see her. Those Mexican prisoners named her "La Luz" for "the Light," but Celeste, she always called her "Lucy." Down on the shelly beach, with Lucy standing guard, Celeste would tell me stories about the ships that had sailed here in the past, the battles fought off these shores, the cutthroats and monsters that dwelled in our woods. She'd pretend to be afraid. But the truth is, as we hiked the island exploring, neither one of us ever got scared. Safest I ever felt in my life was with my big sister.

A gulf wind gust shoves me to the side, and I need to lean hard to keep the cycle from tipping. Celeste's landfall is still twelve hours off, but she's playing games with me. Once I've steadied myself, I spare a glance in her direction and think to my sister, *You'll need to do better than that.*

No doubt this is more evidence for Dr. Jody's theory of my delusional view of reality, something I had to pretend to accept as part of my "cure" just to get out of therapy. Dr. Jody was convinced Celeste's ghost was all in my head, a projection of subconscious guilt or some fancy egghead name like that. But I know the truth. See, me and Celeste always had a deal on those long hikes: We'd stick together. There came a time at the end when I had to leave her, when I didn't think I had any choice. That's why one of the only times I can predict she'll show up is when I head north to Hackberry or Lake Charles. She's always waiting for me at the iron bridge, along the side of the road. As I pass, Celeste always says the same words, the last she ever spoke: *Just stay, Eli! Don't you leave me!* That's something I never told anyone, not Dad or Mom or Father Arceneaux or Dr. Jody.

Up ahead on Infinity Road, I'm surprised to see someone parked on the shoulder. I recognize the familiar Humvee as

I near and pull behind it. With its huge wheels, camouflage paint job, and twelve-foot antenna, a beast like this tends to stand out. The Humvee's owner, Sweeney Soileau, stands off the side of the road, facing the high grass. Tall and lanky as a scarecrow with the creamy brown skin of most Creoles, Sweeney doesn't turn as I approach, and when I get to his side, I see what he's focused on. Nestled in the brush is a wounded deer. The doe's front legs, spindly like sticks, tremble as it struggles to rise. Flattened on the ground, its hindquarters are stained with blood. The deer's ears twitch as it stares at me with big marble eyes, dark brown like Celeste's.

Sweeney pulls off his ratty Saints baseball cap and combs a bony hand through his hair. "What you know 'bout this?"

"I know it's not deer season."

"I heard that," Sweeney says. "Damn thing spooked out of her poor mind. Came across her now just a few minutes back."

Trailing from the doe to the road is a slick patch of wet redness. Sweeney shakes his head. "What kind of sick-in-the-brain you got to be to not finish this job? It's not like she run off in the woods and needed tracking. She right on the road when I come by, waiting to die."

I think of the Odenkirk boys, maybe out for sport on the eve of disaster, but I don't offer any names. "You trying to decide what to do?" I ask.

"No," Sweeney says, tugging his cap back on. "Ain't much deciding at this point. Just working up my grit. When a thing has got to be done, it's best to get on and do it." With this, he strides back to the Humvee, opens the door to lean in. When he straightens, he is holding a pistol. He cocks it on his way back to my side. My gut clenches at what's coming next, and just like with Celeste, I find myself a frozen witness. I don't even blink as Sweeney levels the gun and shoots the doe cleanly in the head. She collapses. Everything goes still and quiet. He spits into the grass and says, "Hellfire."

Even around these parts, Sweeney's known as a bit of an odd bird. He served in the Army Corps of Engineers and claims to have seen combat in Iraq, though plenty of folks think he's making that part up. Others maintain the war is precisely what made him like he is, a bit off-kilter. These days, he's the park ranger at the Chenier Wildlife Sanctuary, which takes up a good chunk of the center of the eastern Shacks.

He kneels now in the grass by the dead deer, and I can't tell if he's praying or checking for signs of life. "I don't figure this at all. Ain't a living soul around, and that bullet wound is fresh. Like the last half hour, if you made me guess."

"Hard to be sure," I say. "Sweeney, what exactly were you doing out here driving around?"

From his knees, he glances up at me. "On patrol. Trouille's raised the white flag, and the island is unprotected save for yours truly. Something mighty unorthodox is unfolding before us. Know them wild hogs everybody says is gone for good? Yesterday I saw three, in a field just past the Chains, setting together staring at the sun. And this morning, there must have been two dozen hummingbirds at my feeder, but not fighting like you always see them. No, they were taking turns. I never heard such a thing. This hurricane's got everything all haywire."

"Sweeney," I say, "the iron bridge is going up at five. The sheriff told you that, right? Everybody is leaving the island. It's going to get flooded by the storm."

He flashes me a smile. "Not my place. I'll guarantee that and sign my name."

Sweeney lives at the center of the wildlife sanctuary in a cabin raised up on I-beams set in concrete. I made a house call to his tree fort back in the spring to fit a new motherboard into a Frigidaire that wouldn't stay cold. "You ready to bet your life on that?" I say.

He seems to consider this for a moment, then returns his attention to the deer carcass. "Something's entirely wrong about this. Entirely. You ever seen an entry wound like that?"

I take a step closer and bend. The bloody hole where the bullet entered the deer's hindquarters looks the same as every other entry wound I've ever seen. But I'm not sure Sweeney's interested in hearing my version of reality. "What are you thinking?"

His eyes tighten in thought, and suddenly he rises, cocking his gun and loading another bullet into the chamber. He scans the empty road and then the gray sky. "The Feds have got drones. Damn fast and quiet as a bad intention."

"Drones?" I say. "Those helicopter things with the cameras?"

"Sometimes they got more than cameras," he says, sparing me a warning glance. "Trust a man who knows."

"Why would the government want to kill a deer?" I ask, realizing too late my insulting tone.

But if Sweeney heard it, he doesn't care. Attached to his belt, a walkie-talkie crackles static, and he listens closely. The garbled message ends. Content that we're not under attack, he relaxes. I feel just a bit bad for saying what I'm about to, but Sweeney's got no business staying in harm's way.

"Maybe you could take the deer up north," I say. "To a lab or something."

He nods deeply. "That's not half a bad idea. They'd have a hard time disputing scientific evidence."

"Right," I say. "Good point." I'm not sure who "they" is, but it doesn't matter.

"I might just could do that," Sweeney says. "Give me a hand."

Together we load the deer onto the hood of his Humvee, secure it with rope. While helping him, I have to stand on the bumper, and I almost slip on the winch attached to the front grille. I helped him use it once to pull a tourist's minivan from a culvert. Once we're done, Sweeney shakes my hand. "I'm glad you come by when you did, Eli. You're a good kid. I don't believe none of what everybody says about you."

I pump his hand and say thanks, then watch him climb into his truck and loop around on the road. He lays on the horn as he drives away, and he raises a fist out the window, an act I'm not sure how to interpret.

After he's gone, I go back to my bike and realize that Sweeney never asked me the most obvious question—what are you still doing here?

A light rain begins, and again I head west on Infinity Road, and in just a few minutes, I reach the Chains. Slowing, I pass the tree where somebody nailed a sign up: DON'T EVEN TRY GOING ACROSS IF SOMEBODY'S COMING. YOU GOT TO WAIT! I head down a fifteen-foot slope like a boat ramp, leading to the quarter-mile stretch of land that links the eastern Shacks to the western. The road itself is no wider than a single lane, with the gulf on one side and the intercostal on the other. Certain times of year, the road washes out during high tide, so I'm not surprised to find the ocean already pushing waves up over the sides, rolling across the cracked blacktop. I take my crossing slow and steady, keeping my tires on the yellow dotted line whenever I can see it through the water.

On the far side, I scoot up the ramp and zip along for a couple miles till I pass the old fort where Celeste used to tell me tales of long-ago battles. When I near that oak just off the shoulder, I try not to look, but my eyes betray me. The damage has healed up over the years, and there's no evidence of the crash. But my mind calls forth a ghostly mirage, and I see Celeste's red truck crumpled into the tree. There I am behind the wheel, twelve years old with a bloody forehead.

I'm glad now to keep going. Not far past the oak, I come up on the lighthouse. Lucy stands tall and dignified in the thin rain. I park my bike in the gravel lot, among the sprouting weeds and the rippling puddles. The cyclone fence is fifteen feet high, put up on my dad's insistence after what happened with Celeste. At the gate, I swing my backpack off my shoulder and read the faded notice about the property being closed to the public for safety reasons. There's also an address where to send donations to help preserve this historical treasure for future generations. An old rusted chain loops through the giant fence and the gate. I drop my pack and unzip it. I spread the bolt cutter's metal jaw and fix it on one of the links, press my grip together so it chews through the steel. Once I finally break through, I need to unwind the chain, which ends up being longer than I am tall. I drop it clanking on the gravel, where it coils like a metal snake.

The actual door to the lighthouse rotted out long ago, leaving only a stony archway. My flashlight casts a white ball of illumination and a spooky glow onto the stone steps that curl along the inside wall. As I climb, I shine the light down on the stairs and listen to the echo of my footsteps. About a third the way up, and then again near the top, I pass tall rectangular windows with the glass blown out, leaving only huge iron frames that remind me of crosses. The slanting rain makes the steps slick near the windows, and the wind rushes through the openings. Up near the very top, I come across a musty smell and some spray-painted graffiti on the curved rock wall. "Shax 4 Life!" one reads. Another proclaims "Heather Loves Blake!"

I sit on one of the last steps and set the flashlight down, aimed up into a square-shaped opening. Used to be you just climbed through there and were in the crow's nest, but now they've got it blocked off with this sort of metal trapdoor. One more project for the bolt cutters. The thick curve of the lock takes more work than the chains did, but after a bit of effort, I finally chew my way through, and it drops away into the darkness. I hear it clatter down the stairs to the ground two hundred feet below.

Even with the lock gone, the door's awful heavy, and I need to shove up hard—shoulders first—to flip the dang thing up and over on the hinges. I climb up into the rustling air of the crow's nest, the round room that caps the lighthouse.

Dead center in the middle of the circle is a thick stump of concrete, all that remains of the base of the actual light. All the windows here are long gone, so the soft rain coming in cools my skin. Looking south, I see the open gulf, normally flat as a sheet of glass. Right now it's a series of small white-tipped waves curling toward shore and crashing over the wall of rocks they dumped a quarter mile out to prevent erosion. Way past that barrier, beneath the covering of gray clouds, the horizon curves softly. That's one of the things I love most about being up here—you can see straight to the edge of the world. Nothing can sneak up on you. Or so you'd think.

The Sabine River, which splits Louisiana from Texas, empties just west of here, and when I look south to the horizon, a half-dozen oil rigs rise out of the ocean. To the east, up past the Chains and halfway to the rigs, I see the *Capricornia*, a paddle-wheel gambling boat. She's sitting in about ten feet of water, depending on the tide. Back at the beginning of the summer, on its way up to Lake Charles from over in Gulfport, the *Capricornia*'s engine erupted. Rudderless and aflame, the boat drifted till it ran aground in the shallows. Apparently, there's a lawsuit about who has the responsibility to haul the boat's wreckage away. Pretty good bet that won't be a problem after tonight.

From here, the only sign of civilization is the water tower, so far east it's just a tiny egg on stilts. I can picture at its base our little downtown, the courthouse, Cormier's Grocery, Zeb's Gas 'n' Geaux, St. Jude's, and that fancy new sporting goods store.

I try to keep my eyes from sliding down, letting them roam everywhere but the place I want to see least. Finally, though, they track down to the rocks piled up at the base of the lighthouse on the beach side. This was the last place I saw Celeste alive, and it's no shock to see her standing there now, looking up at me, whole and unbroken. Like I figured she would, she came to watch, maybe to be a witness herself. Maybe today I can finally give her peace, and her spirit can move on. I listen in my mind for one of her nasty comments, but nothing comes. Maybe there's no point, seeing as how she's getting what she wants at last.

I drop my backpack and dig a hand inside to fish out the last of our beachcombing treasures. I set them in my other palm: the spiraling white seashell shaped like a cone, the green piece of glass worn smooth by the sea, the striped nautilus big as a half-dollar, and the bright blue feather of a bird I never could identify. I lift the spiral seashell, hold it over the rusty railing, and release it. It drops away into nothingness, down toward where Celeste waits on the rocks. I figure that the green piece of glass, which is slightly larger and heavier, might make more of an impact, something I can see at least. But when I let it go, it too just seems to vanish from view, swallowed by the air before it can crash. The nautilus curves like a tiny hurricane, or the lighthouse stairs. When I tilt my palm and let gravity take it, the same thing happens—it just turns invisible middrop. And it's a crazy notion that settles in me, but maybe when I fall, I'll just fade away. Maybe the emptiness I feel at my core will finally spread out and the molecules of my body will come apart from each other and I'll disappear. That doesn't sound so terrible.

Last I hold the feather, four inches long and dark blue. I know what's next, and maybe I linger a bit. As I'm hesitating, Celeste sends a rush of wind, trying to yank the feather from my grip. She's staring up at me in the gentle rain, so light I can barely feel it now. *It'll be okay*, I hear her say, sweet and coaxing. *Just come on.*

I extend my arm over the rail, with the simplest resolve: When the feather hits the ground, or when I can't see it anymore, I'll slip under the rusty rail and follow it.

The moment I release the blue feather, the storm snaps it up. The feather twists into the air, fluttering like a butterfly. It's a freakish wind, something on the edge of supernatural, and it floats the feather around the lighthouse. I follow it along the curve of the crow's nest. Only on the northern side does it finally start to ease its way down to earth. My eyes stay with it only for an instant, though, because a rattling mechanical sound steals my attention. Out on Infinity Road, a quarter mile to the east, a vehicle is approaching fast. Even at this distance, I can tell that muffler needs replacing. Its choking complaint gets louder, echoing over the flat marshland.

The red Jeep pulls into the parking lot, right next to my motorcycle, and the engine and the muffler's growl cut off. The driver's side door swings open and out climbs a tall girl—a real one, no ghost. She glares up at me with her hands posted on her hips, clearly ticked at my presence. At first, I think her hair is colored crazy, but quickly I decide it's got to be a hat or something. What kind of girl would dye her hair green?

Chapter Three

WE STUDY EACH OTHER FOR A GOOD BIT, ME ON THE platform and the girl down below. She leaves her Jeep and crosses through the fence's unlocked gate, then plants herself right below me by the entrance. I can't quite decide if she's real, 'cause I can't figure any reason why anybody would be crazy enough to be at the lighthouse now. If she's some sort of spirit like Celeste, she's an angry one. Even from two hundred feet up, she looks pissed something fierce. But that's not my problem. I came here on a mission of sorts, and spectators weren't invited.

After a bit of this stalemate, both of us just staring at each other, I wave her off, giving her the universal "go away" sign. Either she doesn't understand or she's redefining stubborn. With both hands cupped to her mouth, she hollers something, but by the time the sound reaches me, the words are lost. I shake my head with an exaggerated motion so she knows her message didn't get through. I try waving her away again, this time with both hands, as if I'm shooing an animal. I yell, "Get lost!"

She raises one hand. From this distance, I can't be absolutely certain, but I think she just gave me the finger.

I recall my backpack and yank an apple out. At the railing, I cock my arm, take aim, and hurl it her way. Just before it beans her, she jumps clear, and the apple smashes to bits in the rocky gravel. The girl turns to the pulverized fruit, back up my way, and then she charges toward the stairs.

From up here on the platform, I can hear her pounding up the winding steps. I'm surprised, and a little impressed, that she's not slowing down in the blackness. I don't see the beam of any flashlight, so she's making her way in thick shadows. As she nears the top, her footsteps grow louder and I can hear her breathing hard. Rather than slamming that metal door on her, I back up when she comes into the rounded room, and I'm surprised that, yeah, that hair on her head is neon green. Short and spiky. On top of that, she's got tiny metal balls popping out both sides of her nose. She's winded, sucking air, but even with her hands on her knees I can tell she's tall. Soon as she catches her breath she says, "All right, jackweed, what exactly is your major malfunction?"

Her accent tells me she's not from anywhere within a thousand miles of here. "I'm looking at my only problem," I say. "Tell me something—all the clowns at the circus you ran away from got green hair?"

She straightens up to her full height, nearly half a head taller than me. "You'll have to get in line if you want to make fun of my hair." With her fingertips, she fluffs up the spikes along her forehead. Her nails are painted black.

I ask, "What the heck are you doing here?"

She looks around the crow's nest, as if she only now realizes just where she is. When her eyes find the ocean, they kind of glaze over. I can tell she's instantly someplace else—she takes this long, deep inhale and tightens her lips—but she pulls herself back. "I got business to attend to. How about you like climb back on that sorry antique scooter down below and putter off into the sunset?"

"That sorry bike's a 1987 Ducati Indiana with a 650 cc engine. Probably the only one you'll ever see."

She glances over her shoulder. "Look, peewee, I got a long list of things I care about, and the engine on your cycle sure as hell ain't one of them. You up here trying to earn a Boy Scout badge or something?"

I shake my head. "Don't trouble yourself about why I'm here."

As if it to insert herself in the conversation, Celeste blasts a wind so strong it rattles the roof.

The girl glances up. "This thing safe?"

"For now," I say, "but I can't make any promises."

She cracks half a smile. Like she's an engineer making an inspection, she circles the curved balcony of the crow's nest, one hand running along the empty metal frames of the observation booth. Her face mellows a bit, and I realize she's kind of cute when she's not all ticked off. She says, "This isn't like I remembered."

Now I know where her mind drifted to before. "They've

had this place locked up for a while. That memory's got to be pretty old."

"Eight, nine years," she says. "I was here with my dad."

"Camping? Fishing?"

She throws me a look. "Ghost hunting. We started over in New Orleans, where he grew up, and we ended up doing a three-day tour of the state's best haunting grounds."

This mention of spirits makes me glance down to the rocks. Celeste is walking down the beach, away from me. I wonder where she's going for a second, then turn back to the tall girl. "Weird family vacation. You all find anything?"

She shrugs. "Nothing but what we wanted to."

I'm not sure what that means, so I say, "My name's Eli."

She nods. "I'm Max. Only make a joke if you're really sure I've never heard it before."

Several come to me, but I ask instead, "What's that short for?"

"Maxine. Go ahead and call me that if you want to lose a few teeth."

I can't help but laugh, and Max makes a tight-lipped smile. I point to the slits along her pants, openings wide enough to show skin, and ask, "What happened to your jeans?"

"I bought 'em this way."

"Full price?"

Her smile broadens. "Are you this island's number one wiseass?"

"Pretty much. But I'm not native grown. I'm a transplant

from Houston." I point out to the distant horizon, the oil platforms. "See those rigs? My dad's job moved us here when I was a kid."

She curls her lip and says, "Fossil fuels are killing our planet."

"Everybody this friendly where you're from? Where's home for you anyway?"

"Home?" she asks, and inhales kind of sharply. She wipes at her forehead. "I came down from New Jersey."

Another gale rattles the tower, this one strong enough that we each grip the railing. We step back inside the round room where the beacon used to be and sit side by side, backs against the curved wall. Max says, "I do feel kind of weird. That final stretch of driving was like nine hours straight, and I don't really remember the last time I ate."

I offer her an apple and a granola bar from my pack, which she accepts without thanks. She munches in silence, then asks if I have anything else. I pass her a water bottle and tell her to finish it off.

After she's done, she tosses me the empty and says, "That feels better. I appreciate it."

"Don't mention it."

She gets to her feet, a little unsteady but then gaining strength. She runs a hand along the iron frame of an absent window, looks up at the ceiling. "This old girl's got good bones. Whoever built her did her right."

Without making it a history lesson, I tell her about the Mexican prisoners, as well as the ill-fated preservation project the locals tried to fund. She listens closely, and when I finish, she says, "It's a shame they're letting her fall to pieces. Restoring her would be pretty awesome."

"Be a heck of a job. She's in piss-poor shape."

"I worked with my dad on a special project one summer. A dilapidated carousel at the shore, worse off than this. When we were finished, it was good as new."

Fixing a broken thing provides a certain sense of satisfaction, but making something like it was before, like I did with the old Ducati, that's something else altogether. She comes to the other side of the beacon's foundation and inspects it, like she's trying to figure something out. "They didn't even have electricity when this was built, so how did they—"

"Whale oil at first," I tell her. "Later on, kerosene. The flame was amplified through mirrors and a lens, just like at Alexandria."

"Am I supposed to know where that is?" She asks this in a sort of fake aggressive way, so it comes out friendly.

"The lighthouse at Alexandria," I say. "It was one of the Seven Wonders of the Ancient World."

"Let me guess—sophomore-year school project?"

I shake my head. "My sister loved history. She used to talk about the Seven Wonders, wanted to go back in time and visit them all."

"What do you mean, used to? She stopped talking about them?"

I think of the different ways to answer. "She's gone," I eventually tell her. "There was an accident."

Max looks away. "Sorry, I didn't know."

"That's the past," I say. "Ancient history."

We're both quiet in the awkward space that follows. Finally, Max says, "Well then, I guess we should talk about the here and now. So how you want to figure out our little dilemma? Flip a coin? Rock, paper, scissors?"

"There's nothing to figure out. I was here first. Possession is nine-tenths of the law, or something like that."

At this, she bristles. "So it's your clubhouse and I can't play in it? That's real mature. Look, how 'bout a bit of this southern hospitality? Take off for, like, ten minutes. Then I'll be gone and you can have it back to do whatever you're doing here. How about that?"

For the first time, I hear a sadness in her voice, something desperate. This girl's got a major problem. And I feel it spreading through my chest, the urge to help her fix it. "What are you running from?" I ask.

She grits her teeth and steps into me. "Dude, I don't know your deal, and I don't need to. But don't pretend you know a damn thing about me and don't start playing junior shrink. You got me?"

I don't step back and don't look away. I can't quite tell if she's about to take a swing at me or start crying. But I don't get a chance to find out. A sound turns both our heads. Together we watch two ATVs turn coming in from the west on Infinity Road, turning onto the gravel path that leads to the parking lot.

"Oh crap," I say. "Come on."

As we take the steps two at a time, I aim the flashlight

straight down. The ball of light floats and jumps. Right behind me, Max asks, "You know these guys?"

"Odenkirks," I tell her. "Scavengers. Real nasty. Don't say nothing."

By the time we charge into the parking lot, a quartet of Odenkirks are waiting for us in the slanting rain. Charity, her long matted hair tied back, is wearing dirty overalls and work boots. A senior at our high school last year, she's got the hood of the Jeep up and is peering inside. Closer to us, the two youngest — Perseverance and Obedience — turn our way and square off. Percy is my age, skinny with a thick head of wild black hair. Obedience is bald and thicker, but still just a mini version of Judgment, the eldest. Judge is sitting sidesaddle on my bike, casually appraising it. He's on the far side of six feet and weighs at least twice what I do.

Judge gawks at Max's hair, glances toward her New Jersey license plate, and sucks his teeth. "And they says we're backwards," he tells his siblings. Then he peers at my face and asks Percy, "Ain't this runt the one you tussled with back in the fall? He busted your lip good, right?"

"Sucker-punched me," Percy says.

That's a lie, of course. It was a fair enough fight that got out of hand, leading to one of the times Trouille hauled me in.

Judge rises to his full height. "He's all messed up in the head, yeah? Sees things ain't there?"

"So everybody says," Obie answers, looping a single finger around the side of his head.

Judge chucks his chin down toward my ride and says to me, "You rebuild this here Ducati?"

"I did," I tell him, surprised he could name it.

"Mind if I take it for a spin?"

I'm about to speak, when Max rushes toward Charity, who slams the hood and steps away from the Jeep. The long chain in her fist comes into view. I figure it to be the same one I cut from the fence before, and the sight of it freezes Max in her tracks. Charity rolls her wrist, and the dark, corroded links writhe like a serpent in her grasp. She grins and says, "You're awful tall for a leprechaun." She walks around to the back, casting an inspecting eye. At the rear bumper, she says to her brothers, "Same situation we got—no ball, no hitch. Could be useful, though. As for under the hood, we might could make use of the battery."

"That sound we heard before?" he asks.

"Nothing but the exhaust. No concern of ours."

Judge turns to us with a mocking smile. "Here we was about to drive all the way into town looking for what we need, and from out of the wilderness came a sign, a great cry. We sought and lo! we did find. The Lord doth provide."

The younger brothers nod.

"Listen," Max says. "I don't know what you guys think is going to happen here, but there's no way that—"

Charity swings that chain and bashes it onto the Jeep's hood. The sound shocks Max to silence, and she looks at me for some kind of explanation. Charity pulls back the chain, revealing a nasty scar on the red paint, and says, "If you didn't want for us to take it, why'd you go and leave behind the keys?"

"Speaking of keys," Judge says. Fifteen feet away, he holds out one upturned hand, filthy-fingered, and scrapes at the air.

I turn to Perseverance. "Percy," I say. "Me and you, we had us some misunderstandings. I'm sorry about all that. But you can't just leave us out here, stranded. There's a hurricane coming our way."

Obie rubs rain from his face. "That a fact? We hadn't heard."

Judge starts limping away from the cycle, dragging his right leg. I heard he broke it when he was just a kid, but his mother refused medical attention, trusting in the power of prayer to mend his shattered bone. As he nears me, he says, "This is a time for reckoning. Celeste's wrath will be terrible, it's true. She bears down upon us with ferocious anger and a thirst for holy retribution. Mother Evangeline has known this for weeks, long before science could detect the storm's approach. Such is the gift of vision she receives from the Lord."

I've heard stories about his mother's prophetic powers. Time was when she made a few bucks off gullible tourists, telling their futures and communing with their dead. Now Judge stops five feet from us and fixes me with his eyes. "She tells us that this hurricane will wash away the inequities from this island, but the righteous and pure will remain unharmed."

"What exactly are you trying to say, Judge?" I ask.

"I'm saying give me them goddamn keys or I'll take them." He reaches behind his back. When his hand comes around again, it's holding a snub-nosed pistol. He sees my eyes lock on it and says, "Boys."

Percy and Obie start our way.

"Hang on now," Max says. "Look. I don't know what kind of craziness I wandered into here, and I don't care. But there's something in my car that I absolutely need. I have to have it, you understand?"

Between Max and the Jeep, Charity begins to spin that chain, whipping the rain and making a low whirring sound. "Maybe we absolutely need it too. Ever think of that, cupcake?"

"You don't understand," Max says, almost pleading. "This thing, it's really important." She takes a half step toward Charity, hands up, and Charity stops spinning that chain. There's a sudden softness in her face.

This disappears when Judge fires that gun, aimed just over my head. "I'm fixing to stop being all polite and courteous," he says. "This ain't no negotiation. Time to give up what you got."

Percy and Obie advance, and Charity closes in too, her face hardened once more. Max retreats backward until she bumps into me. The four of them have us surrounded. "Okay, fine!" I shout. I reach into my pocket, grab the keys to the Ducati. I clutch them in my palm and hold my fist low at my side, as if preparing to toss them. "Catch."

Judge smiles, shoves his gun into his beltline, and extends both grubby hands. And I step forward, rear back my arm like a quarterback, and heave those tingling keys over his head, twenty feet beyond the bike. They drop with a plinky splash into the soggy scrub brush, submerged in the advancing ocean.

Everybody turned to follow the flight of the keys, and then Judge brings his face back to me. "Guess what they say is true. That you're a few eggs shy of a dozen." He hobbles up and glares down at me. "But that may have been the craziest thing I ever seen a body do."

The other three Odenkirks inch forward, and Max and I find ourselves back to back inside a huddle of thugs. Percy eases his hunting knife from his boot and holds it up. Seeing it seems to give Judge an idea because he reaches out and takes it from his brother, turns the blade over in his hand. Then he spins and marches to my bike, and I know what's coming. Bending over, he stabs the knife into the front tire, releasing a whoosh of air. He draws the blade sideways, carving a slit. Just for spite, he slashes the back tire too, then comes back to us. He hands the knife back to Percy, who is grinning wildly, and says to me, "I changed my mind about that test drive. I'll have to come back on another day, if that's all right with you."

When I offer only a blank stare for a comeback, Judge shrugs and says, "Guess we're about done here." Percy and Obie head for one of the ATVs, Charity for the other. Judge himself walks toward the Jeep.

"No freaking way," Max shouts, and she lurches forward, but I catch her by the wrist.

Judge twists around, one hand sweeping past his hip and bringing up that gun.

I tug her arm. "Don't," I say, shaking my head. "No point."

Judge tells her, "You best go ahead and listen good to your boyfriend, yeah?"

Max yanks her hand free. She's trying to fight back tears and only barely succeeds. She collapses to her knees as if in prayer. "Please," she says. "I'll give you anything."

Judge looks around, then back at her. "So far as I can tell, Greenie, I'm taking all you got that I want."

Before he can turn to the Jeep, I say, "What the hell are we supposed to do out here?"

"I leave you here same as I found you," he says. "At the mercy of the Lord."

Behind us, I hear the waves crashing over the beachhead rocks. The Jeep leaves first, followed by the ATVs, heading west. Max and I are left alone. The wind pitches higher, and a great sheet of rain washes over us. My drenched shirt is plastered to my body, and my skin chills. This must be from one of Celeste's outer bands, the farthest evidence of her reach. "Come on," I say to Max, who hasn't risen from her knees. "Let's get into the lighthouse and figure out a plan."

"A plan?" She looks up at me, eyes all wide. "What, like 'let's throw the keys away'? A plan like that?"

"Calm down," I tell her.

She stands up, and her knees are muddy with crud. "If not for you, I'd have been long gone by now. This dumb backward island would be in my damn rearview mirror."

I feel the weight of this truth, and I wait for Celeste to appear and judge me. But for some reason she doesn't, and it comes to me that while I failed my sister, maybe I can save Max. "Look now, we got to get our act together. It's six, seven, miles back to the bridge. That's the only way off the island, and it's going up in a few hours. With any luck we'll run into the sheriff or the folks shutting things down. Come on, let's go."

"I'm not in the habit of being told what to do, all right?"

I look up into her face. "I'm not telling you what to do. Just telling you how it is."

She turns her back to me, staring in the direction of the road. Without turning, she asks, "You know where those Odenkirks live?"

The Odenkirk compound is deep in a marshy forest, up on the northern side of this half of the Shacks. But nobody goes back there, and for good reason. I say, "Sure I do. But that's no place I'm heading."

"I didn't ask you to," she says. "Just tell me how to get there." She starts marching, splashing through the puddles that have already formed.

I run after her. "Hang on now. What exactly you think's gonna happen next?"

She stops. "It's not a question of thinking. I'm like that Mother Whatshername. I've had a divine vision of my own. I know you're going to go get that backpack of yours from the lighthouse. We'll need whatever's in it. I know you're going to lead me to where I can find those nutjobs. And I know I'm going to get my Jeep back. That's all there is to it."

Making our way to the Odenkirks' will take a good while, but once I've helped this girl, I'll still have time to double back to the lighthouse, finish what I started. But I'm not going to just give this girl something without getting something. "I might could do that," I say.

She nods.

"But here's the thing," I say. "I'm not in the habit of being told what to do either. I'll get you there, but if we do it, I lead and you follow. That's the deal. And before we go anywhere, you got to tell me straight what's going on."

"What do you mean?" Max asks, tilting into a gush of wind to keep upright.

"What'd you come to this lighthouse for?" I demand. And when all she does is turn away from me and look the white tower up and down, I try, "What's so important in that Jeep that you'd risk your life for it?"

She spins around quick. Something in her face tells me she's deciding whether to be truthful or tell me a lie. In her silence, I try to imagine what answer she might give, but when she finally speaks, it's totally unexpected. "My father," she tells me at last. "Eli, those punks have got my daddy."

Chapter Four

THERE'S NO CARS ON INFINITY ROAD, AND ELI WALKS ALONG the center line, trudging silently through the rain. Ten feet behind him, Max follows with her hands stuffed in her pockets. "How much farther?" she asks.

"Up ahead awhile," Eli answers without turning.

Max sighs. It's not that she's looking for conversation, she's just having a hard time trusting this stranger. Back home in New Jersey, there was no one she felt she could truly count on anymore, nobody she was close to. But something about Eli tempts her to put a little faith in him. Maybe it's the gentleness in his eyes, or the fact that he isn't really trying to be all friendly. That was one of the things that always drove Max nuts about Angie, how she was always pretending like they were best friends.

In the months after Angie officially became her stepmom a couple years ago, her efforts to bond with Max — shopping expeditions to the mall, a disastrous "spa day" — had only made clear the distance between them. Angie was just fifteen years older, but the two of them often fought like sisters. As time went by, her dad learned to stay clear of their arguments, which escalated from stony mealtime silences to stubborn refusal to do chores to complaining about attending church. Max didn't think it could get worse. But six months ago at a diner, Max's dad proved her wrong. That very night, she packed her bags.

The twin Gonzalez sisters convinced their mom to let Max move into a spare room in their basement, where she slept next to the dryer's hum. At first, they tried to treat her like a third sister, and Mrs. G was thrilled when Max installed a bright backsplash in the kitchen and put up some new ceiling fans. But Max cut all ties with her father and Angie, pulling ever deeper into herself. Even the cheery Gonzalezes, always friendly and warm, grew quiet around her. Max wonders if the Gonzalezes went to her dad's funeral, if they, like everyone else, arrived to a panicked Mr. Clayborne and chaos. Max pictures Angie weeping, one hand resting on her stomach, and she turns away from this image, back to the rainy road ahead.

Eli cuts down a rocky path wide enough for cars, and Max looks up to a sign that reads FORT ABENIACAR. There are stone structures, mostly collapsed, but Eli navigates the ruins until they come to a spot where two tall walls intersect and a bit of roof remains, forming a sort of cave. He leans into the corner and folds his arms against the dampness, and she says, "What are we doing?"

"Stopping. There's no sense in us walking into that wind. All we're doing is getting tired and going nowhere. This isn't the hurricane yet, just an outer band, gusting squalls.

They'll come and go all day, getting stronger. I say we give it a chance to let up some and then we move on in the next break."

Max frowns and drops her shoulders. "I say we keep moving." When Eli doesn't react, she goes on, "I thought you said we didn't have much time."

"We don't. But burning up our energy being stupid won't help. Sit."

Max hates being told what to do, but she complies. She locates a rock that had tumbled from the stony wall and makes it a bench. Eli offers her a granola bar from his backpack, but she shakes her head, despite her lingering hunger. She's already in this kid's debt enough. Eli unwraps the foil and takes a bite. At their feet, three inches of water slosh back and forth. "So this is the ocean?" she asks.

He nods and swallows. "The gulf. It's like a big bathtub, and as Celeste pushes this way, the water'll get higher and higher. Just before landfall, they'll be a storm surge, a big wall of ocean water — that'll come on like a huge wave."

"Like a tsunami?" Max asks.

"Sort of. Plenty high enough to drown us good."

"Oh," Max says. "Well, that sounds bad."

"Pretty much bad as bad can be. That's why we've got to get you off this island."

Max wonders why Eli doesn't include himself in the evacuation plans, but she holds her silence, something she's become an expert at. With nothing to do, she instinctively reaches into her pocket for her cell phone, then remembers that not only is it still in the Jeep, its battery is dead. It gave out at a rest stop she'd pulled into outside Mobile, Alabama. Groggy and exhausted from fifteen hours on the highway, she cranked back her seat and closed her eyes.

Then her cell phone hummed. Angie again, this time at 4:00 a.m. Max had seven messages she'd ignored and one blinking bar of power. She let it ring and passed out. When she woke two hours later, the screen stayed black. Max bought some stale coffee and hit the road. Now she wonders what was in those messages. Trying to avoid these unpleasant thoughts, she turns to the mossy stone walls and asks Eli, "So what kind of place is this supposed to be now?"

"Old Spanish fort. Used to be a high wall along the beachfront and a tall watchtower. At one point, they even had cannons, or at least that's what they'll tell you if you pay six bucks for the guided tour. With the beach erosion and all, it mostly collapsed a while back. Nature is patient, but sooner or later, she swallows pretty much whatever she lays her eyes on."

Max can't help thinking of her last glimpse of her father, the tubes in his arms and the beeping machines and his lips dry to the point of cracking.

"So what's your plan?" Eli asks.

Max is glad to leave the hospital. "Plan for what?"

"The Odenkirks. You just going to ask nicely to have your Jeep returned? Way they were eyeing it up, they've got some need for it, so it's unlikely they'll just hand it over."

"I don't need the Jeep," Max says. "Just got to steal back what's in it."

"Right," Eli says. He looks down at the half-eaten granola bar in his hand. "Your, uh, your dad."

Max nods.

"Any chance you'd care to explain that a bit? Just for those of us who can't read minds?"

Max shoots him a look, but he's flashing her a sort of hopeful smile, and it drains the heat from her anger. "I'm talking about his ashes. Like his ashes after he got cremated."

"He's dead?" Eli says, then, "sorry, that was stupid. I didn't know what you meant."

"I stole the urn from the funeral home," Max offers, a little proudly. "My stepmom, Angie, probably had a galactic shit fit."

Eli considers her and says, "A galactic shit fit seems called for. How come you brought it all the way out here?"

Max makes circles in a puddle with her one sneaker. "Already told you. We visited here once, long time back. Spent two nights at a fleabag motel called Kajun Komforts."

"Komforts got torn down winter before last," Eli says casually. "Still, retracing a road trip in a hurricane sounds kind of crazy. What makes that lighthouse so special?"

She offers the same story she told Clayborne back at the funeral home. "On my father's deathbed, he made me promise I'd bring his ashes to the lighthouse. It was his dying wish."

Eli winces and says only, "Damn." Then there's just the slosh of rain against the stony walls.

Max looks at Eli. "You think I'm still crazy for coming here?"

Eli rises now. "Maybe a little bit, yeah. Could have waited till the storm passed. But mostly it sounds like you're being a good daughter, or some close approximation."

She's surprised how these words swell her heart. She's been wanting, maybe needing, to hear someone declare her a good daughter. Even if it's based on a lie.

Extending his hand, Eli says, "Rain's easing up. Let's get to it." His voice is full of heroic resolve, but Max ignores his hand and stands on her own. Eli turns and starts walking, and she wonders what he'd think of her as a daughter if he knew the whole story, about the arguments she had with Angie, the fight that made the neighbors call the cops, the stunt she pulled to ruin their wedding.

Max hustles to catch up to him on the gravel road, sloshing out of the water up onto drier land. The rain and wind have abated, and the sky has a few streaks of bruised blue.

"Okay, so I told you my deal," she says. "Now how about you tell me what you were doing up on that lighthouse?"

Eli turns his face to look at Max but keeps walking. He shifts his eyes back to the road and says, "Nope."

Max wants to ask too about what Judge said, about Eli being messed up in the head, but that will also clearly have to wait. They walk in silence for a while, side by side. She's glad Eli mentioned that Kajun Komforts got totaled. Driving in this morning, she got a little lost in town and was sure she'd stumbled across the location of the old hotel, but in its place was a modern monstrosity, a big, gaudy building shaped like a castle that sold sporting goods. She recalls that final leg of the long trek south with her father, when they retreated from the world after her mother's departure. Each day they'd visit some crappy tourist trap, acting like any other vacationing sightseers. At night, in cheap hotels, they'd watch old movies while Max's dad cracked beer can after beer can till he passed out. Max fell asleep to the TV's glow, afraid to be alone with her thoughts. That whole week, they never spoke a word about her mom, not until the lighthouse.

The cloudless sky outside the crow's nest was the blue of a robin's egg. They gazed together at the sun setting over the distant Texas horizon. Max's dad said, "It's nice up here, the way you can see all around. No surprises. And it's peaceful and quiet. A place like this would be as good a spot as any to have your ashes scattered."

Max knew the time was right to ask the question that had been hounding her. "Mom's not coming back, is she?"

Her dad shook his head. "It's just us now."

He turned to her, and she slid inside his thick arms, planting her cheek against his chest. Then the tears came for both of them, not great heaving sobs but quiet, like a release. Max told him, "Just us doesn't sound so horrible."

Her dad pulled back, wiped at his eyes, and smiled. "Just us is going to be awesome. I promise."

Max nodded her agreement. And somehow, she sees bringing his ashes back to that place as a fulfillment of that promise. *Just us.* When they left the lighthouse, he drove them back home to New Jersey to begin restoring the life they'd lost. Her dad started taking her along on renovation jobs, showing her how to properly handle everything from a socket wrench to a miter saw. After school and on weekends, she helped him salvage properties others wanted to demolish. At night, he began drinking ginger ale instead of Budweiser. When Angie, whom he met later at an AA meeting, first came by their house, Max was happy for him. She didn't yet realize that Angie had come to steal her father.

Without warning, Eli stops suddenly. He glances toward the ocean and then inland. "All right," he says. "This is where things get interesting. Up ahead there's a dirt path that leads to the Odenkirks, but likely as not they'll see us coming if we head straight in. You up for some bushwhacking?"

"Do I have a choice?"

"Not if you want to get what's in that Jeep."

Together they cut across an open field of high grass, with the ground gradually growing less and less solid. As she and Eli near a forest, their feet sink into the mud, so with each step, it takes effort to tug them free. It's like the earth itself is trying to hold Max back. She keeps thinking at the forest they'll find drier ground, but when they reach its edge, she sees the strange truth. The trees sprout from what looks to her like a small lake, with knobby roots jutting out along the muddy shore. About twenty feet from them, something shuffles at the base of one of the trees, and some creature slides into the water and swims away, leaving a V in its wake.

"What's that?" Max asks, stepping behind Eli just a bit.

He says, "Nutria. Sort of like a raccoon-sized rat. Won't bother us if we don't bother it. We'll cut through these cypress and come up on the far side of the Odenkirk compound, if I'm right."

"Compound?" Max says.

Eli hesitates. He kicks a stick out into the water and says, "Where they live, it's kind of hard to explain. My mom told me that way back when—before World War II—there used to be a whole village back in those woods called Evermore. Some hard-core God-fearing religious families came south from Kansas, wanted to be secluded from the evils of society, that kind of thing. They called it a religious community."

"Sounds like a cult."

"Yeah. Anyway, sixty years ago, Hurricane Audrey washed through Cameron Parish, drowned most of the folks in Evermore, and sent the survivors north. For a while, nobody lived out there, but a couple decades back, Mother Evangeline and her brothers showed up with their families, claimed they were descendants, and set about reclaiming what was left. From all accounts, it didn't work out so good."

"What's that mean?" Max asks.

"A fire killed one of her brothers and his wife. Another brother took off after his wife when she ran off. Neither one came back. Both cases, kids got left behind with Mother Evangeline. I also heard her husband got real sick, but she refused to have a doctor come out, said the Lord would provide, and he died. Fact of the matter is, most folks say that woman's crazy as a June bug in July."

Max can't tell exactly what that means, but she knows it isn't good. When she's quiet for a few seconds, Eli bends to retie the laces of his boots. "Might want to be sure yours're on good and tight."

Max follows his lead.

Once he stands and wades into the water, he extends a hand back for Max and says, "Watch your step now."

"I'm fine," she says. "What's with you and wanting to hold my hand?" As she descends, the dark water rises quickly up past her knees, and her feet squish in the mucky bottom. "Anything dangerous in this water?"

"Like snakes and alligators?"

"Yeah."

"Only everywhere."

As she walks, Max's eyes keep darting back and forth. Even though the rain isn't coming down too hard just now, it's enough to splatter the surface of the water. She's convinced she sees eyes in the bumps of a drifting log. A long tall bird, angelic white, bends its curved neck above its watery reflection, then plunges its beak straight down. When it pulls back, there's a tiny fish flipping in its grasp.

Not long after, Max goes to lift her back foot and finds it won't move. She tugs and twists a bit, then hears Eli, who has stopped ahead of her. "Don't force it."

"But I can't move," she tells him, trying not to let on how freaked out she's getting.

"Hang on," he says. "Trust me, you don't want to be barefoot out here." He slides the backpack off his shoulder and hands it to her. Then he puts both hands on her immobile leg. She can feel his fingers working down her thigh, and he kneels slowly into the fetid water. He has to lift his chin to keep it above the surface, and now his hands take hold of her ankle. "Gentle now," he says. "Keep your foot in that shoe for sure. Easy up."

Together they pull, and her foot refuses to budge. For an instant, Max imagines herself trapped here in this swampy forest, and her heart accelerates. "Just dig it out!" she insists.

"Stay calm." She feels Eli's thumbs cram down inside the lip of her sneaker. "Try again." Even the second effort brings no movement, initially. But then with a great heave she's free, and she stumbles back to catch her balance.

When they start walking again, he stretches out his hand, and this time she takes it. It's clammy and cool, but she's glad to have it to hold.

Max loses track of time as they slog along, with Eli guiding her through the cypress maze. At last they reach the far side, and the muddy ground angles up toward the shore. Right where water meets land, Max spies a makeshift dock and a long, skinny canoe. Eli holds up an open hand, scans the area, then leans in. "One of the Odenkirks' pirogues. Stay quiet. Stay close."

She nods, and they pick their way through the knobby roots along the bank. Her soaked jeans stick to her skin, and her sneakers are covered in muck, squishing with each step. Up on land, they follow a waterway that runs from the cypress swamp, an inlet where the water is free of trees.

Just after they come around one bend, an acrid stink curls Max's nose. She sniffs and turns to see something in the air above the bayou. Hanging from a chain looped over a low branch, just a foot above the surface, is a wet carcass of fur and flesh and bone. Flies swarm around the rotting meat. She gags and covers her mouth, turning away and lurching to all fours. The muscles clench in her gut, but she holds steady.

"The hell is that?" she asks.

Eli takes a knee at her side and drapes an arm over her shoulder. In a low voice, he says, "Used to be a nutria. The Odenkirks must be hunting gator ahead of the season."

"With that?" Max asks.

"Gators don't care much for fresh meat. As scavengers, they'd just as soon go after something already wounded or outright dead. Stinkier the better. Even when they catch something, they set the dead body under a log to rot for a few days. Makes it easier to tear up and digest. So that bait's a real treat. Gator'll come along, balance up on a tail, and snap it down. Won't know about the big hook inside or that there chain, attached to the base of the cypress. Later on, Odenkirks come by, see the bait's been taken. All they got to do is tug on the chain and wait with a gun."

"Doesn't seem very sporting."

"It's how everybody does it."

"Everybody? Like even you?"

Eli nods. "Sure. Since I was nine. You gonna call PETA or something? You're in the Shacks now. You've got to change the way you're thinking."

"I'm thinking I'm crazy being out here."

Eli chuckles. "I'm glad you're starting to see the light."

Max falls silent. She sits back and focuses on her stomach, which feels settled. After a minute, steadying herself with an arm on Eli's shoulder, she rises up. But as she stands, her eyes fall on something that makes her gasp. Still gripping Eli's shoulder, she squeezes twice. "Eli," she whispers.

He stands too and follows her gaze twenty feet into the woods, where a pair of huge hogs studies them with unblinking eyes. Eli says just one word, quiet and low. "Razorbacks."

The boars are brown-black beasts, the bigger one the size of a small bear. Even in the rain, clouds of breath mist from their open mouths. Jagged white tusks, dirty and crooked, jut up from their lower jaws, extending on either side of their snouts and wrinkling their lips into snarls. A line of prickly hair sprouts from each forehead and runs the length of their backbones. There's something wrong with the face of the larger one, and Max decides it must have been burned sometime because the flesh there seems melted.

She holds very still, since that's what Eli's doing, and says, "Why exactly are we not running like hell?"

Slowly, Eli turns his head side to side. He reaches for her hand and slides his fingers around hers. "Better to help them figure out we're not what they're smelling. Come on over with me real easy."

They shuffle to the side, away from the nutria carcass, and the burned razorback raises its snout and sniffs the stale air. When it grunts and starts toward them, Max tries to bolt, but Eli holds her fast. "If we walk away, they won't follow. Run, and it's their instinct to chase."

With that, they slowly back farther away, and the hogs advance to the water's edge, where they lift their heads and stare at the bait, out of range. "Keep coming," Eli says. After a few more steps, they turn around, saying nothing. Max is just beginning to feel some sliver of relief when the silence behind them is cracked by a strange sound, the distant barking of dogs. It pierces the swamp air like an alarm. Together Max and Eli turn to the razorbacks, fifty yards away and startled, charging now right at them.

"Go, go, go!" Eli shouts, and he sprints into the woods. Max follows, her eyes searching for a tree with branches low enough to climb. But these trees aren't like the ones back home. Each stark column has no purchase for twenty feet or more. Eli turns again, now circling back in the direction of the riotous barking, and Max can't waste the breath to ask what he's doing. She can hear the razorbacks snorting behind them and gaining ground. But she keeps her eyes straight ahead, and over Eli's shoulder she sees the pack now, a quartet of lanky thin hounds, bounding across the terrain. They snap their jaws and sprint in their direction, locked onto the hogs.

Eli, still running, glances back at her and says, "Don't get between 'em."

Max has no time to warn Eli. Judgment Odenkirk, thick as a tree himself, steps out from behind a cypress dead in their path. He swings something in his hands, and it connects with Eli's half-turned face. The sound is sickening, like a baseball caught flush by a home-run bat. Eli crumbles, and Max barely stops herself from tumbling over him.

Judge's eyes don't go to Max's face but fix tightly behind her. They narrow as he swiftly repositions the rifle on his shoulder and says flatly, "Git down."

Max drops just as the gunshot explodes. She covers her head, and there's a second report. The dogs swarm over her, and she feels their paws pouncing on her back. When she lifts her face, her ears are ringing. Next to her, Eli's eyes are closed, and blood wells from his forehead. She looks up at the Odenkirk boy, who holds the rifle at his side now. He's focused beyond her still, and when she follows his gaze, she sees one slumped hog, motionless, and beside it a writhing mass of claws and teeth. The four dogs, sinewy with thin muscle, are locked in combat with the remaining razorback, which swings its head to gouge the hounds. One leaps in and locks on a leg, and another jumps onto the hog's back, then sinks its teeth into the rear of its neck. The razorback whinnies and bucks, like a bronco trying to ditch a rider. With one tusk, it catches a dog in the side, tossing it yelping into the brush.

Behind Judge, a second hunter jogs up, also carrying a rifle in both hands. This one Max also recognizes from the lighthouse parking lot—the one Eli called Percy. He glances at her and Eli on the ground and says, "Mysterious ways." Then he cocks his rifle and aims it at the remaining razorback. But Judge sets one hand on the muzzle and shakes his head. He lifts his chin and whistles three sharp blasts, and the dogs disengage. They trot timidly toward him, leaving the wounded razorback. Its rear legs are shredded and useless, and it struggles to drag itself away. The big man levels his rifle and shoots from the hip. A moment later, in the eerie silence, Max looks up to see the great boar collapsed.

Now Judgment turns to Max and Eli. He studies them with the same steady gaze he had for the hogs, a look void of emotion. Max thinks he may well just shoot them. Instead, he says to Percy, "The swamps have provided us with abundant blessings. Mother Evangeline will be most pleased."

Judge whistles once more, and the hounds erupt into motion, descending on the dead hogs, ripping and tearing at that foul flesh.

Chapter Five

Whatever it was rang my bell back in the woods did some kind of pretty damn good job, 'cause my brain is pounding something fierce and the world itself is sideways. At least that's the impression I get as I first come to, but then I figure out I'm facedown in the dirt. I go to reach for the throbbing pain in my head, see if there's blood, and that's how I learn my wrists are tied tight behind my back.

With effort, I manage to sit up, righting the world. One eye is swelled mostly shut, but as the vision in my good eye comes clear, I see I'm in a tent, the canvas rattling like sails in a high wind as rain wallops against the sides. Dogs bark somewhere, and there's not much doubt who the dogs belong to, or who's got me trussed up like a roped calf at the rodeo. I tug at my bonds, but my wrists don't budge. When I inch back, my fingers pulling along the rope, I come across the stake it's tied to, pounded into the ground. There's not enough slack for me to kneel, let alone stand.

I wonder what they've done with Max, or if somehow that crazy girl got away. Of course, wandering alone in the swamp with that storm bearing down could be worse than being a prisoner of loonies. Hard to say.

Something sniffles over in a dark corner of the tent, and with a start, I realize I'm not alone. A tall shadow stands frozen, like a spooked deer. My throat is raw, but I croak, "Who's there?"

"Me," she says, and I realize it's Celeste. Only thing that's weird is I can hear her voice with my ears, not just in my head. I wonder why she's chosen now, after all these years, to finally speak to me like this. But I'm just lifted up by the pure joy, so much that the pain in my head disappears.

I say, "I'm so sorry."

"Sorry for what?" she asks, still in the darkness.

My mind flashes to the lighthouse rocks. "For not saving you."

She giggles and moves forward out of shadow, but with every step, she grows smaller, like she's shrinking. By the time I can see her clearly, she's not my sister at all. She's turned into a child, a kindergarten girl, with long brown hair. She's wearing some kind of red dress, a sort of ballroom gown. "Saving me from what?" she asks, and nothing makes sense. With a chubby hand, she twists the top off a bottle of Sprite. "Want some pop?"

I nod, and she sets the bottle top against my lips. When she pours, what comes out is flat and lukewarm. Still, I'm grateful. I ask her, "Can you undo these knots? My hands are really sore."

She seems to be considering this as she returns the top to the bottle, but I don't get the sense she's inclined to free me.

I say, "That sure is a pretty princess dress."

"Not a princess," she tells me. "I'm a fairy."

"I never met a real fairy," I say. "What's your name?"

She raises a single finger to her lips. "If they hear us, they'll be mad." Outside, voices pass by. The girl walks calmly to a wall, bends down, and peels up the side. As she crouches on all fours, she looks back at me and says, "Don't tell nobody I was here, or we'll both get in trouble real bad. I'm Sabine. Just like the river."

Even though my face feels stomped in and I'm a prisoner of her family, I can't help but smile as she slides under the canvas. Almost in the same moment, a big flap gets pulled back on the opposite wall, and dull gray light enters the chamber. I wince and dip my head. "Told you I tied him good." This is Percy's voice, and when I lift my face, I see him and Obie bending over, looking at me like I'm some kind of freak show exhibit at the Calcasieu Fair.

"What happened to Max?" I ask.

"That her name?" Obie asks in return. "She safe."

"I want to see her."

Percy kicks me in the leg. "I want to be King of Texas. I ain't waiting on it to happen any time soon." He kneels behind me and starts in on the rope staking me to the ground.

Obie makes a point of showing me the rifle he's carrying in his other hand. "Don't know what you were thinking coming out here, runt, poking around, trespassing."

Percy stands up and hooks me by a crooked elbow, my wrists still tied. He heaves me up, and I don't really fight.

I need to know more about what's going on, and I'm not learning jack in this tent.

He tugs me out into a steady rain, and we emerge on the edge of a thick forest of scraggly witch hazel and wild buckthorn. The tent's in the weedy backyard of an old-style Acadian log cabin. When we come around the front, plodding through puddles, I see a gas grill alongside an old pinball machine on the porch. It's weird and out of place, but I feel the strange desire to go see it if works. That fairy girl Sabine is sitting in a still rocking chair, watching us walk by. She greets me with her eyes and takes a sip of her soda. The brothers don't pay her any attention, and it passes through my mind what Dr. Jody says about Celeste: This girl might be a figment of my imagination.

Next to us in the compound is a similar cabin, this one in worse shape, with a busted window and a tilted shutter hanging on by a nail. On its porch a little gang of what look like middle schoolers huddle together, passing a single cigarette and staring at me. With a yank, the brothers march me forward, and I see other log cabins, a whole ring of nine or maybe ten more. They're roughly spaced in a great circle with just a couple missing. In one open lot, a lonely stone chimney rises, and I remember the fire that claimed one of Mother Evangeline's brothers. In another lot, there's a blocky RV with a huge satellite dish on top from like 1990 or something. The vines growing up the sides cover the tires completely, but the boxy windshield is still clear. A calico cat curls up on the dashboard. Like all the cabins, the RV faces the center of the clearing, where a hardscrabble church rises from the dirt and the weeds. It's one of those old-timey one-room schoolhouse buildings, where it's easy to imagine folks speaking in tongues, charming snakes, casting out demons. That's where the brothers got us headed.

Halfway to the church, we enter what feels like a mix between a dump and some half-baked flea market. There's a ratty billiard table and a few bicycles, a rusty metal desk and a refrigerator with no door. A telescope on a tripod is aimed into the light gray clouds passing swift overhead. A bunch of golf clubs lie tossed on the ground. We pick our way through a whole zoo of garden sculptures—little stone elephants and giraffes, lions and rhinos, some of them painted cartoon colors. Overgrown azaleas and rhododendrons crowd the outside of the building, edging up over the bottom of the tall, thin windows. Along the church's back, there's this huge silver egg on three wheels, like a tricycle. The front wheel, mismatched, is rigged to the V-shaped metal bars, which makes no sense. I see the words "Airstream Roadmaster Deluxe" on the side and realize it's some sort of camper-trailer. The thing is parked so close to the church, there's no space between them. A thick blue tarp covers the trailer's roof, rattling in the wind.

Around the front of the building, the brothers practically drag me up the wooden steps, and for a second, I see out beyond the circle of log cabins. There's an odd-looking building, a barn tilting at a precarious angle, with the back end of what I think is a white school bus sticking out. Light shines through the wooden slats of the barn, and when I tune my ears, I hear the low hum of a generator out there. Other than this, there's no sign of electricity on the compound. I'd heard these folks were living off the grid, but I didn't know they'd left it so far behind.

Percy kicks open the church's front door, and inside there's flickering light—a few kerosene lamps up by an altar. I see they got two windows boarded up, and from the angled ceiling, rain drips down into a handful of grimy buckets. Four weary ceiling fans with limp blades and an out-of-place golden chandelier hang from the ceiling, suspended by only an orange extension cord. The two dozen pews are mostly shoved to the side, with a few knocked over. Two people stand up together near the altar, a man and a woman side by side, like bride and groom.

"Eli!" Max hollers when she sees me. She breaks away from Judge and rushes down the aisle. I see her hands are tied in front of her—rope wrapped around her wrists—but she loops her arms over my head and we have a kind of awkward embrace where I can't hug her back.

From the front of the church, Judge says, "We's in the house of the Lord. You'd best mind your lustful thoughts."

Max shoots him a look, and the wind rattles one of the windows like a loose tooth. Then she looks my way and her eyes tighten. "Your face."

"Somebody did a number on me," I say.

Judge strides up to us, hobbling on his stiff leg. When it broke, did they pray for it to mend in this very place? He puffs up his thick chest. "Maybe it ain't smart, you charging through the swamp. Never know when you'll run into somebody's rifle." He shrugs and at his side, I see the Remington he's holding.

"Yeah," I say. "That's sound advice."

He grants me a toothy grin and takes in my shiner, admiring his work. From the feel, I'll bet it looks about like an eggplant.

Behind him, there's a loud voice — almost a shout — from the other side of a red curtain covering the left wall of the altar. The three brothers trade a look. Obie lifts his chin, making a question, and in response Judge shakes his head. "That girl had best watch herself. She's messing with heresy."

Max interrupts them. "Can't you guys at least get me a towel and some water? His face needs to be cleaned."

Judgment huffs. "That boy's face ain't on my list of things to worry about."

Our odd little congregation makes its way to the front pews, and Percy shoves me down onto a pew. Max sits next to me. Judge limps around the pulpit and plants his elbow down as he leans forward. "So good to see new friends with us to worship the Lord." Percy and Obie laugh, drop into the front pew across the aisle, kick back, and cross their legs.

Behind Judge, the four kerosene lamps flicker on the edges of a foldout table in the altar space, giving the air a bitter smell and casting a bouncing yellow glow. It falls on three statues, each life-sized, along the back wall. The Virgin Mary holds a baby Jesus, and a bearded man rests both hands on a mighty saw — Joseph the Carpenter. The third is Christ himself, complete with a crown of thorns. He's raising one arm up like Father Arceneaux does when he delivers a blessing. Only that arm's hand on the statue is snapped off at the wrist, so it's just the stump and empty air. I feel the strange need to draw this sight, catch it on the page. Like the chandeliers, it clearly doesn't belong in this place, and I wonder what church up in Lake Charles or Sulphur is missing its holy family.

The voices on the other side of that curtain rise up again, making us all turn. One voice is low and even, almost hypnotic. The other spikes sharp and snappy. Obie says, "They going at it pretty good."

Indeed, the one who's shouting is getting loud enough now that I can make out some of her words. "How 'bout the kids . . . impossible . . . a few hours, maybe. It'd take a miracle." The brothers are trying to listen too, and while they are distracted, I ask Max in a low voice if she's okay.

Leaning into me, she whispers, "I'm fine. Nobody hurt me or anything. These people, they're insane."

"I thought I'd brought you up to speed on that."

Without warning, the red curtain splits in two like on a stage, and Charity stomps through, still wearing overalls. She looks surprised to see us, but she doesn't say anything. After a hesitation, she heads for the aisle, and Judge scoots up, blocking her path. "Mind you keep a civil tongue in that brazen head of yours."

Charity flashes him a challenging look.

A sharp bell rings out from the room where Charity was, and the air in the church shifts. Charity shoulders past her big brother, and as she moves through a patch of lantern light, wetness shines on her cheek. When she passes by me, I see her fingers are black with grease. Part of me wants to ask what sort of engine she's trying to fix.

After she's gone, Judge tells Obie and Percy, "Get on after her. See what help she needs." The younger brothers stare at each other, and Judge goes on, "I can handle these two." When he sees me looking, he lifts the Remington from his side and holds it like a threat.

The younger brothers are clearly ticked to be sent off, but they do what they're told. Max helps me up, and that bell rings again, impatiently. Judge goes to the curtain and peels back one side. He tilts his head into the shadows and says to us, "C'mon, now."

A weather-beaten wooden sign just inside the doorway reads MOTHER EVANGELINE. SPIRITUAL ADVISOR AND MEDIUM. CASH ONLY. When I pass through the curtain, I nearly stumble, but Max steadies me from behind. The floor drops down a few inches, something that helps me realize we're inside that silver egg trailer. They must've hacked a wall out of the church proper and made this flimsy addition. The room we step into feels like a good-sized cave. Like the church, it's lit by lanterns, with a half dozen spread on top of the antique dresser, the nightstands, and a huge rectangular box leaning weirdly in one corner. There's also a loud ticking from a grandfather clock, though when I look to see what time it is, I find one hand is missing.

As for Mother Evangeline herself, she's propped up in a four-poster bed against the far wall, beneath a frilly canopy that reminds me of something you'd see in a dollhouse or an old black-and-white movie. She sits up with her back against the headboard, with a bright red scarf covering her hair. On either side of her, pillows support her plump arms. A tray with a box of tissues, some bottles, and a small silver handbell with an ornate handle waits on one side. "Come closer, children of God," she says. "These old eyes don't work so good."

Judge shoves us from behind, and only when I'm close enough to touch the bed do I see the circular glasses set on her chubby face. A blanket covers her lower half, though I can see the mounds that must be her belly and legs.

She smiles warmly and says, "How I been waiting for you." Here she's looking not at me but at Max, and something like pleasure is clear in her wide eyes. Max just nods and says nothing. Mother Evangeline waves a thick hand at us and tells her son, "There's no need for them ropes. Our guests will behave themselves, won't you?"

"Yes, ma'am," I say.

"That's a bad idea," Judgment says. "They's both a bit wild."

Mother Evangeline looks at Judge briefly, then turns to that tall box leaning in the corner. "When did all this happen, Aloysius? When did our babies begin to doubt me so?" In the dim light, I see a small cross carved about three-quarters of the way up that wooden box. Shifting back to her son, Mother Evangeline says, "You'll pay heed to the fourth commandment. When you honor me, you obey the Lord."

Judgment unsheathes a knife from his belt as he moves behind me. He roughly grabs my tied hands and yanks them down so my shoulders snap back and I'm pulled straight, and I feel a tension in the rope, then a rip. Freed, I rub at the chewed-up skin of my wrists and see him turn the knife he's holding to Max, who lifts her bound hands. He cuts her loose and whispers to me, "This here's my hunting knife. Blade's plenty sharp. Bear that in mind."

"Young man," Mother Evangeline says, "show us that face." I cross to her and lean in close, one hand on the plushy pile of blankets. She inspects me. "That wound wants cleaning."

She nods at Judgment, and Max can't help giving him an "I told you so" look. He shuffles into a side room and returns with a basin of water and a cloth. He puts these on that tray setting on the bed, which I see now is dirty yellow and plastic, probably swiped from our school cafeteria. Mother Evangeline has me sit on the edge of the mattress. Gently, she begins to dab at my forehead with the damp cloth. She says, "What brings you to my home?"

"Listen," I say, "we only want—"

"Not you," she interrupts me. "I want to hear from her."

We all turn to Max, standing at the end of the bed. She shrugs and says, "I'm just trying to get my daddy back."

Mother Evangeline wipes tenderly at my cheek. "That so? And where is your father?"

"In the Jeep your creepy kids stole."

"Stole?" she says, and her voice sounds offended. She holds the washcloth steady, contemplating something, then continues. "It's a sin to covet. My children salvage those things that others discard. We collect here the unclaimed and unwanted, the flotsam and jetsam. Isn't that right, Judgment?"

"Yes, Mother," he says. "Flotsam and jetsam both."

She goes on, "When you found that abandoned Jeep, was there a man in it?"

"No, ma'am."

She finishes with my face and drops the cloth in the basin. "That's better. The swelling will go down in a couple days." She tilts her head back and considers Max through those tiny glasses. "My boys aren't prone to lying."

"My daddy's dead," Max says. Her words make Mother Evangeline go stiff for an instant. I swear even those lamp flames pause, then dance again. A hard gale outside whistles loud, and the floor shifts as the trailer rocks just a little. Mother Evangeline motions for Judgment to take the basin away and stares hard at Max.

I say, "You really think she'd just abandon a Jeep?"

"In the face of God's wrath, it's not unusual for many to shed their material possessions. The physical world is a shackle itself, binding us to this unclean place. Even our bodies are nothing more than rotting prisons from which only death, the great liberator, can finally free us."

Max says, "See, now that's something I know a bit about. My dad just got liberated a few days ago."

Mother Evangeline asks, "And how did this come to pass?"

"Cancer. In his pancreas. Around Memorial Day, he noticed he was losing some weight. By July Fourth, he was admitted to the hospital. He never left."

Plucking a tissue from the box on her bed, Mother Evangeline looks at the coffin. She wipes her eyes, then turns back to Max. "You have our condolences and sympathies. The path God asks us to walk is not without sorrow. The great rupture of death shatters our lives. Isn't that your experience, young Eli?"

I'm caught off guard, but I recover quick enough. "My experiences aren't something that need concern you."

"I do not judge you like the others. Quite the opposite. Aloysius has stayed behind with me, much the same as your sister's spirit has lingered."

Max asks me, "What's she talking about?"

I'm not sure what to say, and Judge jumps in. "Your boyfriend didn't tell you his sister's ghost follows him around? Years back, she took a tumble off that lighthouse where you two were making naughty."

I grab the washbasin off the bed and swing it into Judge's face. It catches him flush on the cheek with a satisfying clank. He recovers fast and lifts the rifle up like a bat.

Mother Evangeline yells, "Not in the Lord's home!" and Judge freezes.

There's an odd stillness then, and I can see in Judge's face that his pride was stung when I caught him off guard. Finally, it's Max who speaks. "We weren't making out," she says. "Anyways, we aren't talking about Eli and his sister or whatever. We're talking about me and my dad. His ashes are in a shiny silver can that was in the Jeep. I want it."

Mother Evangeline nods as she processes this. "The trophy? Yes. Charity brought that to me earlier. We were curious about what it was, and she's quite fond of it."

"Where is it now?" Max demands. "It's mine."

But Mother Evangeline looks over at the coffin. "Be patient, Aloysius. I will ask her." She smiles at Max. "Do you ever have strange dreams, child? Waking dreams that speak to you of the future?"

"Can't say I do. Sounds like a hoot and a half, though. You going to tell me where my dad is, lady?"

Judgment leans toward her. "You'd best learn to tame that tongue. Or somebody's likely to tame it for you."

"Just give us our stuff," I say.

The tone in my voice must be enough for Judgment, who swoops in behind me and grabs hold of my shoulders. Mother Evangeline lifts up a plump hand, and I say, "Let us take what's ours and we'll drive out of here, never look back. I'm trying to get this girl off this island before that storm hits. I don't even know what time it is, but it's got to be getting late in the afternoon. That iron bridge goes up at five. Trouille told you all this, right?"

Mother Evangeline nods her head as if listening. She glances toward the coffin and grins. Finally, she says, "We cannot overlook God's providence. He provides for His children the things that they need, even when they, in their eternal ignorance, don't comprehend His divine and holy plan. God put that Jeep in the path of my family because we have need of it. Returning it to you now would violate God's plan, and so I cannot do that. Also, I cannot allow you to leave this place because God wants us to face the storm together."

Max rolls her eyes and shakes her head. "I take it God tells you His plan."

"God reveals His plan to all who listen. But through His grace, I have seen that which lies ahead. You have visited me before, girl, with your green hair and your venomous words. In my visions of what is to come, I have foreseen our shared fate. We are bound together. Only the most foolish try to resist the will of God."

I can't believe this. All my life, I heard the Odenkirks were a bit extreme, sure. But what I'm seeing today, the way she's talking, it's a whole other level of nutjob.

"What you fail to realize is that you stand on holy ground. This church was sanctified by my ancestors, who watch over us still. My great-grandmother was blessed by visions that brought her and her followers to this place from this country's farmlands. But the children of their children were weak, and in their weakness, they abandoned God's gift and fled this island. They betrayed their blood and denied their destiny. They failed their test, and now God, in His infinite mercy, has given us a chance to make amends. He has spoken this truth to me that we face a trial. It may come to pass that His wrath will claim these homes. I know the waters may rise up. But He will spare the island. And the faithful who remain shall bear witness to His greatness. They shall be lifted up and considered His most favored servants."

Soon as Mother Evangeline finishes her mini sermon, Max goes to speak, but I cut her off. "It's no use, Max."

But Max can't help herself. "You're telling me you're going to risk the lives of all your kids on account of what a bunch of dead people did? Lady, that's ancient history."

Mother Evangeline strains to sit forward. "The past is never the past. The dead don't never die. We are chained to what was, the same as our souls are chained to the flesh."

She's quiet now, and there's only the wind outside and the rain splattering on that blue tarp draped over the Airstream's poor excuse for a roof. The hole above us is big enough that if God reached down, He could pick Mother Evangeline right up. Her gaze slides from Max to me. "Would you, blessed by visitation from your own departed sister, deny the truth of my words?"

Judge and Max wait for me to speak. The camper shimmies in a strong gust, and I look down at the unsteady floor. "I got nothing to say."

Mother Evangeline seems to consider this. Then she says, "Very well. I am grateful for this chance to visit. Some of my children are preparing a great feast, which we'll enjoy together in the church. With the glory of what's to come, a celebration is called for. For now, you both have much to contemplate." She lifts that thick chin toward Judge. "Take them to the tent.

Then check on the others. Be certain your sister is all right and that her work is proceeding."

Judge aims the Remington toward the door, but I don't move. "Mother Evangeline," I say. "I'm good with machines. I could help your daughter with whatever she's trying to get running."

Mother Evangeline tilts her chubby head toward the coffin and nods. "We see your true plans, boy. Sabotage and flight. It's more difficult than that to deceive those who stand with God."

I shrug. Honestly, I was trying to help save them too.

Judgment ushers us toward the curtained exit. But at the threshold, Max puts a hand on the frame. She turns back to Mother Evangeline and says, "What is it exactly you want me to contemplate?"

"The coming of the King, child. He descends upon us with the storm, with the wind and the rain. He comes to test our resolve and sound the depth of our faith. And I for one will not be found wanting. You must decide for yourself how best to prepare. The day of reckoning is at hand, and you and I are surely fated to confront it side by side."

Chapter Six

PRODDING THEM WITH THE BARREL OF HIS RIFLE, JUDGE marches Max and Eli back across the compound, hobbling crookedly behind them in the steady rain. When Max looks at Eli, he seems preoccupied with a sound coming from a slanting barn down below, a whining grind of an engine that won't crank over. The wind blows a ragged kite along the ground, and it reminds Max of a wounded bird struggling to take flight. Max is amazed by all the junk and crap scattered everywhere. She can imagine a time when the buildings of this bizarre compound may have been sturdy and proud, but that was decades ago. Now, with the rot and mold, Max is pretty sure they can't be salvaged. Could be a case where tearing them down is the right thing, starting with a clean slate.

At first, she's not sure why this thought brings Angie to mind. Max remembers how badly she treated that woman when she first began dating her dad. The nasty looks and the snide comments about her appearance, her youth, those goofy AA coins she was so proud of and that shiny gold cross she always wore. Max couldn't believe someone could be so sincerely optimistic, though she's pretty sure that stealing the urn will have wiped that ever-present smile from Angie's face. But just now this notion gives Max no pleasure, and some part of her wishes she could go back in time and have a fresh start.

The truth is, as much as Max hates to admit it, Angie was good for Max's dad. She helped him stay away from the booze and used her contacts as an interior designer to get him some good upscale reno jobs. But Max begrudged the way Angie would always ask about her schoolwork, her grades, and her plans for life after high school. Max was certain that Angie's lectures about college were motivated by a desire to ship her off, out of state even, just to have Max's dad to herself.

At the edge of the Odenkirk compound, Judge takes them through a ring of log cabins to a tent just inside the tree line. Max sees some kids up on the porch out of the rain, watching them as they go. She wonders where they came from, where their parents are.

Without meaning to, Max lets this troubling thought slow her pace, and Judge jabs her in the lower back with his rifle's butt. She trudges on.

Inside the tent, Judge makes them stand back to back and binds their wrists, then ties them together. He steps back to admire his handiwork and says, "I'd set you face-to-face, but then there's no telling the kind of trouble ya'll would try to get into." Eli says something Max doesn't quite hear, and Judge kicks him hard in the hip, toppling them both to their sides in the dirty grass. As he leaves, he says, "Be nice and maybe we'll take you with us."

Once he's gone, the two of them wriggle until they're at least sitting up, backs pressed together. Max has so many questions—about Eli's sister, her fall from the lighthouse, the haunting that apparently followed—she's not sure where to begin. But she finally chooses a more recent curiosity. "What do you think Baldy meant by that?"

She can feel Eli's hands trying to undo the knots. After a bit, they go still, and he says, "I knew there was a difference between crazy and stupid. Down at that barn, they got a couple vehicles, I figure. They're working on some way of getting the family off this end of the Shacks. The land out here is practically below sea level. When that storm surge hits, it's sure to flood. I just can't reckon how they expect to move Big Momma. It doesn't look like she gets out much these days."

"Who cares about Big Momma? Or any of them? Let's make a break for it. That tent flap isn't locked."

She hears Eli sigh. "You want to go for a six-mile hike in a hurricane tied back to back? Maybe I'm the first to tell you this, girl, but you got a serious problem with impulse control. What we need is a plan, first part of which might be getting free."

She feels him tugging again at the knots, and she starts doing the same. But Judge spent a while with the ropes, and they seem tight as cords. When Eli finally stops, she asks, "How's your face feel?"

He leans his head back onto her shoulder. "About like a piece of stomped meat. Last thing I remember is running from those hogs. What happened after I was out?"

Max pictures the hounds, how they snapped and snarled at the great boar and tore it to shreds. She had never seen anything die before, and the beast fought till the bitter end. The way that razorback whinnied and wailed, it reminded her of a child's cry. The whole way back to camp, the brothers kept the dogs on leashes, but they strained against them, lunging at Max. Now and then here on the compound, she's heard their raucous barking. She won't admit it, but she's terrified of them.

Instead of telling Eli any of this, she says, "What you'd expect. They killed those hogs, then dragged us back here. Judge carried you over a shoulder. He's one strong SOB."

"Thing about big guys like that, they aren't used to being hit. If you can tag him good in a fight, just sting him, it tends to screw with their minds. You see his face back in Mother Evangeline's bedroom?"

She relishes the memory, wishing only that she had flung that pan at the big man herself. Speaking back to back with Eli feels strange but nice. Max eases her head onto his shoulder and rests it there, just as he's doing, so they're cheek to cheek, looking up into the tent's darkened peak.

"I never should have brought you here," he says. "It was a dumb idea."

"Dumb for sure," Max tells him, "but tell the whole story now—the idea was mine."

"No. I knew who these people were. We should've just hiked up to the bridge. Who knows? By now, maybe we'd be across the intercostal."

"What time do you think it is?"

"Hard to tell with the storm blocking the sun, but if I had to guess, around three maybe? Four? How should I know? I'm the one who was knocked out, right?"

Max laughs gently. Outside the tent, they hear two voices pass by, and Eli smells cigarettes. After the voices are gone, Eli says, "Okay, now. If we're going to get out of this, you need to trust me. Don't forget our deal. I lead and you follow."

"I'm not so good with the trust thing. Everything about this is so royally freaking wrong. What's up with Aloysius?"

"You saw that coffin, yeah?"

"I did," she says. "I was really hoping I had that wrong." And she hesitates, worried that if she goes on, she might isolate her one ally. "I want to trust you, Eli. I do. I need to, I think. I just . . ."

He lifts his head from her shoulder. "What? You got something to say, say it."

Max takes a breath but stays silent. Angie was always urging Max to "express your feelings, especially the bad ones."

Eli says, "Listen good. You and me, we got no time to get to know each other, and we don't have to be best friends. But if we aren't straight with each other and don't work together, the future looks short and ugly."

"All right," Max relents. "The brothers, the way they talk about you being messed up in the head. And Mother Evangeline made that crack about you being acquainted with the dead."

"So?"

"So what's up with your sister?"

The wind sucks at the sides of the canvas tent. She hears him exhale. Then he asks, "You're upset that these crazy people think I'm crazy? All the problems we got on our plate, and that's the thing that's got your stomach in a knot?"

Max inches her tied hands along the ground, awkwardly craning one arm so she can get a grip on Eli's fingers. She squeezes and says, "I just want to know who I'm dealing with here."

As much as he can with the ropes, he yanks his hand from hers. "You're dealing with Eli LeJeune, the Official Lost Cause of Shackles Island. Six years back, my big sister Celeste and me were up at the lighthouse in the crow's nest, right where you and me were." He pauses and takes a big breath, and Max wonders if she heard that right, that Eli's sister shares a name with the hurricane. But that doesn't seem nearly as important as the weight of the words she can tell are coming next. His voice is barely a hush when he says them. "She went over the side, down onto the rocks. Figure since then I haven't exactly been real good company."

Max pictures that lonely lighthouse. She's still not sure what business Eli had up there in the storm—she can tell there's more to this story—but she's closer to the truth now. The silence from Eli is heavy, and she turns her face to the side to say, "I'm so sorry."

Still looking away from her, he huffs, sniffles, then clears his throat. "No point in you apologizing. Nothing you did wrong."

Max feels like she may be trespassing now, but his voice is thick with hurt. And somehow, this conversation, this sharing of secret things, is easier when they can't look at each other. She asks, "But you, you think you did wrong, don't you? I can feel it. How come?"

"What's it matter to you?"

In this crazy place, where it seems like the world really may come to an end, it feels easy to let some secrets slip. "I got guilt of my own," she says. "Know how I told you about my dad's dying wish to have his ashes spread?"

"Yeah."

"That's not entirely one hundred percent accurate."

"You care to give me a math lesson?"

She closes her eyes. "Well, it's true that I finally visited him when he was sick and dying in that hospital. My stepmom had told me about this bad final turn he'd taken, said he was asking about me. But I was so angry and mad still, guilty too, I just didn't want to face him."

"Guilty for what?"

So many examples crowd her mind. Quitting the basketball team. The nose studs. The time she stole Angie's phone just for spite. But one example presses forward. "I dyed my hair green the morning my dad and Angie were getting married."

"No you didn't," Eli says.

"Did too. Just to be sure everybody knew how I felt."

"Were they upset?"

"That's just the thing. My dad sort of snapped, but Angie put a hand on his shoulder, told him it was nice I was putting effort into finding my own look. Of course, that just pissed me off more, so I sulked up the aisle in my stupid gown and sighed and huffed through most of the ceremony . . . right up till that moment when the pastor asks if anyone has reason these two shouldn't be married."

"Get the heck out," Eli says, letting loose a chuckle.

"I didn't actually say anything. I just stood up and walked out — dropped my bridesmaid's flowers in the aisle and everything. My dad followed me out into the parking lot and put the ceremony on hold for fifteen minutes. I refused to go back inside."

"World-class drama queen, huh?"

Max came to this conclusion some time ago, in the hard days after her dad's diagnosis, but hearing it from Eli stings. "Tell me something I don't know now. Once they were married, I tried living with them for a couple years. Nothing but fights. Slammed doors. Smashed dishes."

"Sounds like a nightmare."

"Wait. You'll never guess the last straw. About six months ago, right around Valentine's I remember, Dad tells me he's taking me to lunch at this diner we used to always eat at before he got remarried. Big special deal, just me and him. Alone at our corner booth, he brought up our visit to the lighthouse, how nice it was to be together." Max pauses here. She recalls *Just us* and the connection they'd found at the lighthouse, which is way too hard to put into words.

"Go on," Eli urges.

"He put his hand over mine on the table and said, 'It would be good for us to get back to the lighthouse.' I knew what he meant—the way we used to be closer, like when we visited here, but I didn't see a way to do it. Still, it meant a lot that he was even saying it."

Max goes quiet again, and Eli has to ask, "So how was this bad?"

"Right then, he got this weird smile and told me Angie was pregnant."

"Damn," Eli says. "Bet that felt like a bomb."

"Total nuclear. I couldn't deal with it. I packed my things and moved in with the only friends I had. I refused to answer the phone when he called." Max swallows, trying to keep from getting emotional. "For months I cut all ties. No contact. Angie actually had to drive over to the Gonzalezes' to tell me about his diagnosis in July. Pancreatic cancer. By the time I finally got my head on straight and went to see him at the hospital . . . his body was still there, but his spirit had long since slipped away."

She goes quiet for a while, gathering herself for this last push. "So the thing is, in the hospital he never said anything about the lighthouse and spreading his ashes. All that's been my idea, really. And me, I didn't have a chance to say good-bye or ask him to forgive me for being so self-centered. So yeah, I'll get to carry that around now."

Behind her, Eli shifts. She's shocked by how much she said, how it all came out in a rush. Maybe the truth was like anything kept locked up—it wants to escape. But now, after the release, she feels something like relief. Only, she wishes she could see Eli to read his expression. As she's thinking about this, he asks, "Did you say the words?"

"What?"

"Even though he was out of it in that hospital room, did you say the things you wanted to say?"

Max remembers that terrible bedside, how the metal guardrail felt cold on her chin, how hard the linoleum was on her knees. Her dad's hand in hers, limp.

"I did."

"Then you got no way of knowing what he did or didn't hear. Besides, if you two were out looking for ghosts way back when, that sounds like you believe dying isn't exactly the total end. Could be your dad knows now how you feel. You know, like from the other side."

Max warms at the idea of this, but it seems too easy. "Maybe," she says.

For a while, it's quiet in the tent. Max realizes Eli never told her his whole story, that her tale kind of took over, but he doesn't seem to mind. She feels exhausted, flattened out. Without thinking about it, she finds herself leaning back into Eli again, letting her head dip once more onto his shoulder. Her breathing slows, and she tries to imagine the hospital scene as she wishes it would have unfolded after her confession— with her father's grip tightening on hers, his eyes opening, and the gentle words he would have offered, not just forgiveness but absolution.

She's nearly asleep when Eli asks in a low voice, "Max, all those haunted places you and your dad went to back when you were a kid . . . did you guys ever, you know, hear anything? See anything?"

"Like what?" she asks sleepily. Her eyes are still closed.

"Like proof. When you were ghost hunting."

She rolls her head side to side. "Nah," she tells him. "Nobody proves things like that. Mostly people see what they want to see."

Eli's quiet, and Max lets the silence sit for a while. Then she says, "You want to tell me about this sister of yours?"

Her only answer is the storm. The wind lashes the tent, and Max pictures the whole thing being sucked up into the sky. It feels like forever since she slept, and that was just a nap of sorts at that rest stop on I-10 just outside Mobile. She's exhausted, all but passed out. So she barely hears Eli when he finally says, "Not particularly."

Later—she can't tell how long—Max wakes to Eli's voice saying her name, low but excited. Something taps the back of her skull, and as she comes to, she realizes it's him, reverse head-butting her gently. "C'mon, now," he says.

She blinks back the last of the sleep and sees the reason for the urgency. Standing before them in the tent is Charity. She's still wearing greasy overalls, but now she's clutching a knife in one hand. In the other, she holds Eli's backpack. "You two want to get out of here?" she asks.

"Hell yes," Max says, and she starts trying to get to her feet. "Let's go."

But Eli stays where he is. "Hang on," he says to Charity. "How come you're doing this?"

"Maybe being charitable's in my nature," she answers. "Or could be I'm interested in making a bargain." She sets down the knife and unzips Eli's backpack, pulls out the urn. "Sign of good faith," she says, setting it on the ground.

"What do you get out of this deal?" Eli demands.

Charity kneels down and trims away Max's bonds but leaves Eli tied. The instant her hands are free, Max grabs the urn and stashes it in Eli's backpack, which she slides over her shoulders. "Eli, come on."

He shifts on the ground, hanging his head. "I want to know what she wants in return. Nothing's free."

Charity crouches by Eli and peers into his face. "I'm going to bring Greenie here out to a 4x4 I got stashed on the edge of our property and aim her toward town and the iron bridge. Might still be time to get off the island if you go now. It's closing in on five. I don't need but one of you, though. You want to stay here, that's on you."

Max leans over and says, "You know I've got a better chance if you come with me. What are you doing?"

Eli shakes his head. "Max, something's weird about this. I don't trust her."

"Then trust me," she whispers, her face near to his.

After another moment, Eli nods. "So be it. But I'm telling you, something don't smell right."

Charity saws away at the ropes. The three of them stand and Charity says, "It ain't but a little ways to the 4x4. Everybody's down at the garage, so likely as not we won't see nobody. Just the same, put your hands behind your back, like they's still tied."

They interlock their hands. As they follow Charity toward the tent flap, Max stops. "Hang on a second. What about the dogs?"

"They ain't gonna bother with us."

"Are they chained up?"

"They're down with everybody else."

Eli lifts his chin. "What you got in that garage?"

Charity considers this, then wipes at her forehead, smearing a slur of grease over one eyebrow. She grins an uneasy smile and says, "I'm working on Noah's ark."

"Sounds to me like Noah's got a problem getting the engine to turn over."

Charity glares at Eli, then says, "Rain's pretty heavy now. Stay close." And with that, they slide out into the storm.

As they skirt along inside the tree line, back behind the log cabins, they don't encounter any of the other Odenkirks. They bend against the thickening rain, which seems to be coming at them sideways through the trees. Even with the branches above, when those heavy waves come down, Max thinks she's never felt rain like that back in Jersey. She wonders how close that hurricane must be.

As they leave the compound behind, Max and Eli stop pretending to be tied up and walk one in front of the other, following Charity on a thin trail snaking through the cypress woods. The ground is soggy and hard to see in the half dark. It occurs to Max that this could all be a trap, like in prison movies when the bad guys shoot the convict trying to escape.

Before long, they enter a small clearing by a dirt road. In that open space waits a muddy 4x4 with knobby wheels, maybe one of the same vehicles Max saw back at the lighthouse. On the seat there's a Hefty bag, and for an instant, Max thinks Charity has gathered supplies for them. But then the bag shifts, turns, and Max sees that in fact it's a little girl, the one who looked at her before from the porch. Draped in her garbage bag poncho, she's clutching a ratty stuffed animal, so mangled it's hard to tell if it's supposed to be a bear or a bunny or a dog. On the child's head is a red football helmet—three sizes too big—with HACKBERRY RAMBLERS emblazoned on the side.

Max says, "Now what the hell is this?"

It's Eli who answers. "Sabine?"

Charity turns to him. "How you know her name?"

He walks over to the girl. "What's she doing here?"

Through the face mask, Sabine's eyes float over all three of them, as if she herself is wondering this very thing. Charity says, "She's my favor. You got to take her with you 'cross the bridge."

Sabine says, "I'm supposed to stay with you, Mommy."

"Don't call me that," Charity says. "I'm your cousin, not your momma."

"No way," Max says, backing away. "I'm not gonna be in charge of some kid. She'll just slow us down. No way. It's probably kidnapping."

"You ain't kidnapping her," Charity says. "You're saving her."

Eli's chest expands as he takes in a big breath. Max sees something shift in his eyes as he stares at the girl. They've taken on a strange shine. He says, "Max. Charity's right. We should take her."

Max says, "Now who's jumping the gun? She belongs with her own people. We're going to have enough trouble getting off this island ourselves. We've got to think of what's best for us." She knows how selfish this may sound, and she feels judged by the way Eli and Charity look at her. She asks, "Why don't you take her?"

Charity hangs her head. "My momma, crazy and stubborn as she may be, she needs me. With all my little cousins, we got over a dozen kids out here. I got the old preaching bus running all right, but the Ford truck I'm dealing with, she's ancient and finicky. I'm trying to piece together something with parts from your Jeep, jerry-rig the starter—and I'm close. But the radio says this storm's moving all kinds of weird ways."

"My Jeep," Max says, imagining it in pieces. "Why didn't you just drive out in that?"

"Not near enough towing power for what we need to haul," Charity explains. "I couldn't talk Momma into calling for help, or letting Percy drive the kids north in the bus ahead of us. She says the Lord insists we all stay together."

Max asks, "So once you got this Ford running, you're going to make a run for the bridge?"

"No, no," she says, shaking her head. "That'd be way too sane. Just town. Momma says the higher ground will be enough. She says God don't intend for any of us to leave the Shacks."

Eli lifts his hands, palms up. "Higher ground? In town? This island's basically flat."

"I got no argument with you." Charity shakes her head again. "We got some real young ones here—Judge's kids, plus a handful left behind by my damn uncles few years back when they hightailed it. Sabine here, she's kind of unclaimed. I usually look out for her. But I can't now, so that's why you got to take her. She's the littlest. Plus, she's . . . different."

They turn to her, huddled inside the shiny black plastic of the garbage bag. Max asks, "Different how?"

"Different in all kinds of ways. Give me your word you'll take care of her, and I'll give you the key."

Max turns to Eli. "Forget this. Let's just take off."

Eli puts a hand on her shoulder, which is trembling with the chilly rain. "We'd never make it hiking back to town. It's near six miles, and the iron bridge might already be up. Plus, just look at this kid—she's a scared little girl who needs our help."

"I ain't scared," Sabine insists, clinging to her soaked stuffed animal.

"And think it through, Max. Say by some miracle we get across the bridge. Then we're on foot with another six miles easy up to Hackberry."

Max shrugs, surrendering to his logic.

Eli bends down in front of Sabine. He points at the stuffed animal and asks, "Who is that?"

She extends her arms with the plushy sock toy. "Jasper. He's a muskrat. Mother Evangeline sewed him for me herself. He's magic. Nothing bad can happen to us as long as I have him with me."

Eli nods. "That's good to know. You hold Jasper tight." He turns to Max. "We'll put her in between us, so you're in charge of that backpack for now, okay?"

Max looks down at the ATV, where the rusted chain Charity beat her Jeep with is wrapped around the headlight.

Eli holds out an open hand, and Charity drops the key in his palm. He climbs behind the steering bar and tells her, "I can't be sure, but from the sound of it, I don't think the starter's your problem at all. Give that flywheel a look. I'd guess she's missing some teeth. If you put a file to it, you might advance the timing enough. Maybe."

Charity steps back and nods.

Sabine clambers up behind Eli, and Max sees Charity looking at the girl. Max surprises herself when she says, "We'll take care of her. I promise." Then she settles on the back of the

ATV seat, reaching around the girl to hold Eli's hips. Under her breath she says, "This all just seems like a desperate plan."

Eli cranks the key. "Right about now, desperate's what we got to work with."

Chapter Seven

RACING EAST ON INFINITY ROAD, SLOSHING THROUGH FLOOD-
water, I shouldn't be smiling. Not with this wild windswept
rain swooping in left and right, swirling around like Celeste's
decided it's her number one mission as a hurricane to knock
this little ATV into a ditch. Not with the dark clouds overhead
finally opening up, releasing great downpours of raindrops
like millions of tiny bombs. In between each assault, there's a
quick spell of calm, just enough so you can get a good breath
and think maybe that's the last one. Then another deluge,
and it's a lot like being underwater. Charity's ATV is a total
piece of crap, and even if we weren't out of our minds driving
through the opening act of a Category 5 hurricane, I'd still
need to fight the steering to keep it straight. Oh yeah, and of
course there's no way of knowing if that bridge is still down or
if we're stuck on this doomed island.

But even with all that, I can feel my smile, so wide across
my face that my cheeks hurt. Because right now, with Sabine's
tiny arms wrapped tight around my waist, with Max behind
her pressed into me too, I'm sure in my purpose. This feels

like the flip side of the way I felt before, up on the lighthouse. The hopelessness that settled in me then, the emptiness of that other Eli, it seems like somebody else's nightmare. It feels like the world, or fate, or God has seen fit to give me another chance. *This time*, some inner voice whispers, *you'll get it right*.

The gulf has swallowed the beach whole and made its way up to the edge of the street. Each wave that comes in runs a little deeper up onto the asphalt. I've got the headlight on, and a weak beam shines out into the gray, showing me lines of driving rain.

As much of a rush as I'm in, I'm trying not to go too fast. Me and Max don't have helmets, and a wreck's the last thing I need.

Sabine's tiny arms stretch all the way around my belly, where her fingers fold together, like she's praying. From the way back, Max cups her hands over my hip bones, and I can feel her squeeze tighter when the ATV fishtails a bit on one curve. She hollers, "Careful!" and I'm sure she wishes she were driving.

The only reason I know we're coming up on the Chains is because of the hand-painted sign along the side: ROAD FORMS ONE LANE. Right at the sign, before the road dips, I pull over and let the engine idle.

"Why'd you stop?" Max hollers into the storm.

I drop my boots into half a foot of standing water and point ahead of us. "See the road there?"

"No," she yells.

"Me neither," I shout back. "Now you know my problem." The gulf has claimed the Chains, burying it with the tide. "I was worried about this."

Sabine says, "Jasper wants to know what's wrong. He's getting really upset."

Max faces the stuffed animal. "Jasper, don't worry. Everything's going to be all right." She doesn't sound convincing.

Gray as it is, I can't make out the far side of the Chains. There's no reference point for me to aim at to keep straight. "If we drive off the side, we'll tip for sure," I offer to no one but myself.

"I can't believe the road is gone," Max says.

Sabine giggles. "It's not gone, silly. It's just under the water."

Max taps my hip. "Kid's got a point." With that, she climbs off and sloshes up to the tree line, ignoring my yelling at her to get back. For a minute, she disappears into the darkness, and when she returns, she's holding a walking stick. She comes up close to me and says, "Don't crowd me. But stay close."

I'm not entirely sure what she means, but then she walks into the dull shine of the ATV's single headlight. She gathers herself for a second, then real slow starts forward, swinging the stick along the road under the water like a blind man.

"She's brave," says Sabine, leaning around me to have a look while still clinging to my waist.

"More like insane. But it'll do." I throttle the engine and stay about a car length behind Max. She wades along, the water ebbing and flowing from her shins to her thighs with each wave. As she gets more confident, her speed picks up, so I need to go a bit faster. The knobby wheels chop and churn the foamy water like paddle wheels on an old river steamer. I try to keep the headlight shining in front of her, and it catches on something bobbing in the water. Max holds up a hand and hustles forward, bends down for the dark shape. When she straightens and turns, she's holding a small red cooler, the kind an oil rig worker might use for lunch. With a shrug, she heaves it back into the water, where it plunks and floats away. But then it rises up, higher than it should be, lifting in the dark like it's levitating. By the time I holler for Max, she's already high-stepping back my way. I reach over the handle-bar for her with both arms just as the rogue wave sweeps in. My two hands lock on one of her wrists, and I can feel her weight taken up by the water as it tries to drag her inland. Her face, panicked, disappears in the wash as she goes under, and the wave sucks hard at her body. But I don't let go of that hand.

Just that fast, the wave's gone and I'm reeling her into me. She clutches me around the shoulders, and I squeeze her, giving her a kind of hug around the backpack. Then she bends, plants her hands on her knees, and hacks out a mouthful of gulf water. When she straightens, still wobbly, she says, "That was the storm surge?"

"'Fraid not," I answer. "Just its baby brother."

Max shakes her head and kind of grins at me. She puts both hands on the steering bar, leaning into it for support. I tell her, "If you'd have gone in, I'd have come after you."

I say this without thinking, but I can tell it touches her in an unexpected way, like she's not sure what to do with it. She looks off, toward the girl. Sabine's got her doll tucked inside her garage bag poncho, only its scruffy head popping through the top. She says, "I had a baby brother. When my daddy left, he took him. But me, I stayed with the others. Me and Jasper and all the rest."

This seems to land funny on Max, as a far-off look crosses her face. But whatever it is, she brushes it away and says, "Maybe we should go back, just get to solid ground."

But I shake my head. "We're nearly halfway across, just as close to the side we want. Besides, road's too narrow for me to turn around. Hang on now." I climb into the water up to my knees and help Max slide up to where I was, at the controls. With my hands on her shoulders, I can feel her shivering, and it's not just from the chill. She's rattled good. I place her hands on the steering bar. "Twist here to give it gas." I untangle that rusty chain wrapped around the headlight, loosening one end. I unwrap a few feet of it, leave the rest attached, then walk out till it's tight, like a leash. I nod at Max and add, "Don't run me over."

I start inching ahead in the dark water, staying steady with each sloshing wave that slaps into my side. Here and there I sweep my foot along in front of me, and a couple times I find the edge of the road and shimmy back to the center. It feels like I'm walking through a swirling thick gumbo roux.

The first thing my eyes actually can make out is the silhouette of the scuttled *Capricornia*, a dark black shadow on a dim gray horizon. It's nearly a half mile out, but that acts as a landmark and helps me figure out just where I am. About fifty feet and ten minutes later, I can see signs of the far shore.

I look back at Max and yell, "Almost there!"

Sure enough, with every step, the road starts rising up, until by the time we get to the ramp at the east end of the Chains, I'm kicking through only a half foot of surf. I guide Max up onto the shoulder and wrap the chain back around the headlight. After we take our original positions, sandwiching the kid, I twist my wrist to shoot us forward once again down Infinity Road.

On the eastern side of the Shacks, the gulf is high but at least where it belongs, down by the beach. Compared to where we were, it's smooth sailing, and I accelerate through the slanting rain. We veer left and pass a dozen houses along the intercostal, all boarded up and dark, and then the northern edge of the Chenier Sanctuary. Not long after, we pass the turnoff for my home, and a mile later, we hit the outskirts of town. None of the streetlights are lit, and even the traffic lights are dull, rocking wild in the wind like buoys on the ocean.

You go your whole life hearing a phrase like "ghost town," and you never really give it much thought. But as we pass by the water tower and Cormier's Grocery, past the Sleep EZ Hotel and Leroy's Lounge and the All-Rite Washeteria, we don't see a soul, just sheets of rain washing empty flooded parking lots.

I turn left and bring us along Buccaneer Boulevard, where homes line the intercostal. The choppy water washes over people's empty boat launches, swamps the shoreline decks with four-foot waves. Somebody's Adirondack chair bobs violently along the water's edge, and a rainbow beach umbrella gets sucked out of a backyard, up into the twisting gray clouds.

I keep squinting into the rainy darkness, eager to catch a glimpse of the iron bridge. It's Max who sees something first, and she lets out a bit of a yelp and squeezes my sides. "It's still down!" she cries. "We're gonna make it."

The thrill that rushes over me is like a high I can't describe — I've saved us — but lasts only a few seconds. Then I see the skeleton structure and feel the heavy sag of the truth. Instead of trying to explain, I go ahead and take the turn onto the entryway, swinging us around the lowered crossbar. Max must've seen the section of the bridge attached to the island side, the section we're driving along right now. The tires make a buzzy hum as they race along the grillwork. Below us, the intercostal waters churn. For this brief stretch, we're aimed in the right direction, true north, and I imagine Max's heart lifting with hope. But it's not long before I'm forced to pull over, and I feel her hands go soft on my sides. The ATV's weight shifts, and then she's on her feet at my side, looking up into the storm.

"Screw you!" she yells.

The iron bridge isn't like most drawbridges, split down the middle into two sides that tilt like ramps. Instead, there's three sections — one on each side that stays locked in place and one in the center that can be raised on towers, like a capital H. That raised section is what Max and I are looking at now, maybe fifty feet straight up, high enough for sailboats or the occasional snooty yacht to pass under. It leaves a gap in the road about a hundred feet across. We can see over that empty space to the other side, where the road leads to safety. Right now, those hundred feet may as well be a hundred miles.

I get off the ATV. Holding on to a guardrail, I walk close to the road's edge and look down. I've never actually seen whitecaps on the intercostal, which is normally smooth as a pond. Max says, "We'll find a boat. Somebody left behind a canoe or something."

"We'd capsize for sure," I tell her. "You want to be in that water? Let alone with the kid?"

We both look back at Sabine, who's clutching Jasper, huddled in her Hefty bag.

Max leans in close so the girl can't hear. "Better than waiting for that storm to drown us, don't you think?"

"You're not thinking this through, Max," I say, which draws me a pretty nasty look. But I go on. "Figure we somehow do make it over, and somehow scramble through the swampy crud on the far side, which by now is probably like three feet of thick mud. Then we get to the road and what? We start walking north? It's six miles to Hackberry. We're in a hurricane now. It's going to get a lot worse before it gets better. No way can we be out in the open."

She looks at me, and I can see the light fading in her eyes. "So we die?"

"Maybe not," I tell her.

When I was a kid, I was friends with the iron-bridge guard. He was an old skinny guy from Arkansas named Dallas, and he'd sweat away the day in his booth on the far side, listening to talk radio, reading mystery novels, and aiming his face into a tiny fan. I'd ride my bike to visit him, and he'd pay me fifty cents to bring him a cold Coke and some Lucky Strikes from Zeb's Gas 'n' Geaux. I always bugged him to let me operate the bridge, but he told me he'd get fired. After he decided to retire, on his very last day, he invited me inside the booth and gave in to my request. Dallas let me punch the buttons that activated the blinking red lights and lowered the crossing guardrails. He even let me turn the key and lift the lever that raised the bridge. It was big, but I could shove it up with just one hand. I remember being surprised at how easy it all was.

"I'll climb over," I tell Max.

She gives me a curious look. "Over where?"

When I aim my face at the booth on the far side, her eyes follow mine and she says, "Who's the impulsive one now? No way. That wind'll blow you off like a dead leaf. That's suicide."

That word falls heavy on me, and for just a second, I consider what she's saying. But when I search myself for the sad impulse that made being gone an option, I can't quite find it. Before, I was nothing more than a kid brother who screwed up. Now, with these two relying on me, I'm a guy with a chance to save the day.

"It's the only way," I tell her. "Our best chance. Once I

reach the guard booth, I'll lower the bridge. In fifteen minutes, we'll be long gone."

She reaches for my hand and holds it in hers. "Your face is all busted up. How do we know you didn't get a concussion? I should go."

I shake my head. "You don't know how to drop the bridge. It's got to be me."

She's quiet while she's looking for a way to change my mind, a better way. There just isn't one. When she realizes this, she shrugs. "I don't like splitting up."

"You got to stay with her."

As one, we glance back at Sabine.

"You said you'd follow my lead," I tell Max. "That was part of the deal."

Max plants her hand on her hips, then looks up at me. "This deal sucks."

The section I pick to climb looks a lot like a ladder. There's two metal beams a foot apart, and in between them, crisscrossed, are pistols like the buccaneers used to use. This decorative touch was done to honor our pirating past, something people might regret if they really thought about it. When I reach up high and take hold of one of the barrels, it's chilly and slick, but it makes for a good handhold. I hoist myself up and plant a boot in the cradle of the first set of guns.

As I climb, the rain washes over me, dumping buckets on my head, and the wind tugs at my soggy clothes. The one good thing is that it's shifted to a constant gust, strong for sure, but easy to take into account as I measure when to release my grip and when to hold fast. Plus, I'm on the inside of the girder and the wind is pushing me into the metal. It feels good to be taking some action like this, and I imagine Sabine and Max down below, watching me rise. I don't look back, though. I keep my eyes lifted toward the prize. My hands aren't bleeding, but they're getting plenty chewed up. Red-black rust coats the buccaneer pistols, so it's like I'm squeezing metal sandpaper, and each time I take hold, I can feel its bite.

About halfway to the raised section, as I lift one boot, my planted one slips from its hold. I drop down a foot, but my hands grip tight. My shoulders burn with the strain, and my face bounces into the girder, igniting the tender bruise. My feet scramble for purchase and find some, and as my legs take the weight, my arms ease up. I take a minute to pull myself together and decide not to check if that's blood or rain in my one good eye.

I get back to work, climbing fist over fist, and after a while, I find myself directly underneath the raised section, which makes a roof over me and blocks some of the rain. Plenty still comes at me from the sides, but it's nice to catch half a break. Only problem now—and one I hadn't really counted on—is that in order to get up on top, I need to swing around to the outside of the girder, out over the water. This looks to be tricky business, as the beams are too thick to wrap my hand around. I reach around and get a sort of awkward reverse grip on the corroding guns, then slide one foot around and lock it in. Basically I'm hugging the ladder from the side, but I'm steady enough. The wind picks up, just a bit, like the storm's decided I'm worth noticing again, a genuine threat to the way she wants things to be. I clutch the metal, press my body and face into the beam. She's pulling at me good now, blowing at me from the front and sucking from behind. I close my eyes and think what Sweeney said before he ended that deer's suffering. *When a thing has got to be done, it's best to get on and do it.*

Celeste inhales and the wind lets up, and I bring my second hand around, then carefully my foot, and the switch is complete. I'm outside the structure of the bridge now, with about five feet to go till I can scoot under the railing of the raised section. But Celeste is ready, ticked at the idea of me nearing the summit. My ears fill with her howling, and suddenly the wind is whipping at me from all sides, tugging and yanking. I squeeze so tight that I crunch the rust, and a tiny shower of metal dust sprinkles my face, spiking my one good eye. On instinct I lean away, just a bit, and the wind rushes into that small open space, forcing my chest farther from the bridge. My arms and legs get stretched, but I keep my grip, and I'm like a sail now, anchored by my feet and my hands but otherwise blown back. This gale can't last, and I'll finish the climb, no doubt. It feels strange to be this confident, to feel so certain of my coming victory.

But you'll never make it, Eli. Celeste's voice rings clear in my head. And I'm not surprised to look up and see her there, standing on the raised section and looking down on me. Same as always she's a masterpiece charcoal sketch, cast in black and white, but I can see the disappointment in her almond eyes.

She shakes her head like she's not sure why I even try. *Give up*, I hear. *You just don't have what it takes.*

Maybe I holler her name a few times, and maybe it is I start crying. I don't know. But suddenly I feel twice as heavy and the wind rips twice as fierce, snapping and yanking. The weight of how I've failed before settles in my bones, and my arms ache with the sum of all my defeats.

It's only another few feet to the top. With just a little more effort, I could roll under the railing. The climb down won't be nearly as hard, and in fifteen minutes, me and Max and Sabine, we could be free. All I have to do is pull it together and get past Celeste.

But I find I can't go on. My legs and arms are paralyzed. I'm suddenly terrified that if I let go and attempt to climb, I'll fall. Above me, my ghostly sister hears these thoughts, and her voice echoes in my mind: *Would that be so bad? Isn't that what you truly want?*

Maybe it's hearing the actual question, just laid out like that, but my answer is no. I yell, "I don't want to give up!" Celeste's face twists with anger, but I'm holding tight. I release one hand and stretch up, trying to rise. A blast of wind sweeps in hard, hits me like a baseball bat to the chest. My free arm flails out behind me. But my other grip is firm, fingers clenched around the X of the crossed pistols. As I struggle to secure my loose hand, I feel something strange in my grasp. Just a bit, the pistols seem to wobble.

In the next instant, I'm holding the corroded guns in my hand, snapped free from their rusty girders. Even more insanely, the iron bridge is growing smaller in my vision. I've been blown back, away from the superstructure, skyward. Celeste stands calmly at the railing, watching me get sucked up into the darkened heavens.

Chapter Eight

Down below on the bridge, Max watches Eli get swallowed by the storm. That's what it seems like to her. One instant, he's clinging to the girders like Spider-Man, forty feet above her and Sabine, nearly to the raised section. The next, he's aloft, blown into the open air, arms flailing as if he's trying to figure out how to fly. A blink after that, he's gone from view.

She rushes to the edge, where the road drops away. Beneath her, the turbulent intercostal waters thrash like a living thing. No sign of Eli. She runs now to the bridge's side and bends in half over the railing. Here too there's only the foamy and jagged waves. Panicked, she's all but forgotten about Sabine until the little girl appears next to her. She points skyward. "He went up in the air," she says. "Just like a angel."

"Oh, God," Max says, more curse than prayer. "C'mon!" She grabs the kid's wrist and yanks her back to the ATV, hops on, then guns the engine and swings back toward the island. Max barely slows to maneuver around the lowered guard arm, skids on the rain-slicked street, and then races around the curved road that leads down to the waterfront. She scoots up the first driveway she comes to and hauls straight through the yard, chewing out chunks of soggy grass. "Stay here," she yells at Sabine as she jumps off.

Max rushes onto a floating dock, the sections of which buckle and kick like a sidewalk in an earthquake. She peers into the dark waves, shielding her eyes from the rain with both hands and straining her vision to scan the waterline. She charges into the next yard and the one after that, passing picnic tables and hot tubs and aboveground pools, till eventually she's under the bridge and on the wrong side, far from where Eli would've gone in. There's nothing.

The thought of being alone out here drives Max to her knees. And even though she understands that it's hopeless, she cups her hands to her mouth and screams "Eli! Eli!" Her throat goes raw, and still she yells. Then, finally, she gets up and plods back to the ATV.

She finds the kid on the patio, red-helmeted, tucked up on a deck chair in a few inches of water. Sabine says, "Where did you go like that? Jasper's really scared. He thinks we should break in someplace. We got to get inside."

"Tell Jasper he's got the right idea," Max says. She needs to lean hard into the wind to keep from falling, and it keeps shifting direction. "But this isn't the right place." Without knowing its name, Max pictures their destination, the building she drove by in town when she was trying to find the lighthouse this morning. It was in the lot where the hotel she stayed in with her dad used to be. The new place, a store, looked like a fortress.

She sets Sabine on the ATV and climbs in front of her, then pulls the girl's arms around her as if securing a seat belt. She zips back the way she came, up the gently sloping road. Following the same path they took this morning, but slowed by the storm, she makes her way into town, through the main intersection. She glides underneath a bouncing stoplight, extinguished, and a fill-up station called Zeb's Gas 'n' Geaux. Closer to the beach, she passes a barbershop and a trailer with "Daq Shack!" spray-painted on the vinyl side. There's a half foot of water everywhere now, and Max remembers watching a movie set in Venice, where the buildings seem to rise from the ocean.

Soon, she's reached her objective. The tall gray building is supposed to resemble a medieval fort, Max supposes, complete with an exterior that looks like enormous stones, turrets rising from the corners and, most important to her, a tall central tower, stretching fifty feet into the air. Out front, a sign proclaims THE SPORTSMAN'S CASTLE. The whole thing seems wildly out of place next to the sun-beaten smaller shops along this pitiful wannabe boardwalk.

She pulls right up to the entrance, where an archway rainbows over the front door, covered in plywood. Sabine says, "There's an alligator that lives in the moat of this castle. Be careful."

Max says, "Okay, honey," not really paying attention. She dismounts and finds twin handles for what must be a double door, jutting out through sawed-off openings in the plywood. When she tugs on them, they don't budge.

Taking Sabine by the hand, she starts splashing around the castle wall, looking maybe for a bathroom window that didn't get boarded up, anything. The store backs up to the gulf, and Max isn't surprised to find the tide way up over the beach. High above, she sees the tease of the unreachable tower. Max has never liked damsels in distress, whether they come from fairy tales or Disney movies, but she finds herself wishing Eli were here. Or if not him, a good crowbar. This tower is her goal, the highest ground she can hope for.

At her side, water up to her knees, Sabine seems to sense her desperation and asks, "So that boy's gone?"

"I think so," Max tells her. The second sentence, that he probably drowned, she doesn't say.

"Maybe he'll be back," the kid says.

"Maybe so," Max says, not sure if she's imagining Eli's return as a ghost or in the flesh. She leans into her knees, doubled over like a runner after a race, and is certain of only this: Right now, they are on their own. This child is hers to take care of. The rain beats on Max's bent back.

When she lifts her head, her eyes catch on something beyond the side parking lot. There's a tall black fence, one that looks like the bars of a prison cell, and she wonders what kind of medieval gimmick this is. Driven more from curiosity than anything else, she wades over. The fence forms a large rectangle, nearly the size of a basketball court. In its center there appears to be some sort of mound, an island that even in normal conditions would be surrounded by a ring of water just inside the fence line. This is a cage, Max realizes, something meant to imprison and hold.

She follows the bars around to the front, which isn't all that far from where she parked. And there she comes across a sign that reads IVORY THE ALLIGATOR. It explains that albino alligators are rare, and because their unique pigmentation undermines their natural camouflage, they don't survive long in the wild.

"I seen Ivory before," Sabine tells her. "Charity let me look at him when we were getting groceries at Cormier's once. It's free to just look."

"That's fine," Max says. She watches the ocean waves rollicking through the bars, and she wonders if alligators—albino or not—can survive in salt water. It's not her problem, she knows that, but letting a creature die like this seems cruel. Max walks the fence till she finds a gate just around the corner from the sign. With the tide, the gate swings back and forth on its hinge. If she wanted to, Max could slip inside the pen. For a second, she wonders if some animal lover came and broke the gate down so Ivory would at least have a chance, but then the more practical truth asserts itself. Surely an albino alligator is precious, too valuable to leave behind in disaster's path. Surely when the Sportsman's Castle owners evacuated, they took Ivory along with them.

Looking at the black gate, pushed open and inward, Max sees an image spark to life. Together she and Sabine hustle back to the ATV. Only when Sabine tries to climb on, Max sets a hand on her shoulder and shakes her head. "I got to do something to get us inside. Just wait here."

Sabine says, "Please don't go away again!"

Max slides behind the controls. When she turns to answer Sabine, she sees the child's need in her eyes. Max isn't used to having someone rely on her, and the sensation, though unwelcome, also brings with it a burst of motivation. "I'm not leaving you, kid. I wouldn't do that. Go over by the wall there and just sit tight."

Sabine, cradling Jasper, does as she's told, and Max gets to work. She steers the ATV up to the front door, then unwinds the rusty chain from the headlight. In her mind, she's picturing a scene from a cheesy Western her dad loved, when John Wayne was wrongly imprisoned in the local jail. He summoned his faithful horse with a whistle to the window, then tied its reins to the bars. When the horse backed up, it ripped the metal frame right from its brick housing.

Standing over the front of the ATV, she searches for some way to attach either end of the rusty chain to the doorframe. With no other option, she unwinds a few feet of chain, loops it around one door handle, then ties a knot.

Max climbs back into the driver's seat and slowly reverses, taking up the slack in the chain. Then she revs the engine. The chain trembles with the strain, but the door is unyielding. Max brings up the throttle as high as it will go, until the engine's throaty roar is clearly a complaint, with no luck. She eases back and tries something else. Slowly, she inches the ATV forward, nosing up to the door. This time she jolts backward all at once, accelerating like a starter off the block. Her head snaps forward when the chain catches, a kind of reverse whiplash. She goes ahead and speeds back a second time, even a third, yet the door doesn't seem to notice.

Max can feel the tightness in her eyes that comes before tears. Determined to make one more attempt, she nuzzles the ATV close to the door, then guns the engine full bore, launching the ATV violently backward. There's a momentary hitch, and she's ripping through the water into the parking lot, away from the Castle. When Max looks up, the door remains exactly where it was. She leaps into the water and feeds the chain through her fingers till she finds the end. The knot she made holds tight to the door handle itself, yanked free.

Sabine appears at her side. "I don't think that's working so good."

"No," Max says, her fear turned to anger. "But I got a Plan B." She curls the chain back around the headlight and sits at the controls, then reaches for Sabine's red helmet. "I need to borrow this for just a second."

The helmet is tight, but Max shoves it on anyway. Her eyes are fixed on the wood protecting the double doors thirty feet away. She hunches low to make herself smaller, grits her teeth, braces herself, then revs the engine and launches straight ahead, suddenly riding a battering ram. The ATV sprays water in its wake like a Jet Ski. She's now driving at high speed toward a solid wall.

When she slams into the door, the whole ATV bucks and Max goes airborne, spinning over the seat even as the ATV careens sideways and forward. She's inside. A sharp spike of pain flares along her spine as she crashes into a row of shopping carts and down into the shallow water. Everything goes still. If she blacks out, it's only for a few seconds, and then she hears, "Hey! You wrecked real good!"

Max sits up in the water, rattled but recovering. Smiling, Sabine stands over her with Jasper. With effort, Max tugs the helmet off, then reaches for the straps of the backpack, wincing at the ache the movement causes. She drops it on her lap, the weight from the urn solid and heavy. Max inhales and exhales deeply, testing to see if any ribs are broken, but she finds breathing easy enough. She looks around and locates the ATV, on its side and rammed into a customer service counter. A sign reads NO RETURNS WITHOUT A RECEIPT! At the store's entrance, there's an open rectangle of gray light where the door used to be. Higher water rushes through at the base.

"C'mon," Max says, getting first to her knees and then to her feet. She's dizzy, and when she tries to straighten, something stings the muscles along her backbone. Bent like an old woman, she hobbles forward, ankle-deep in rising water. Sabine slides under one arm to support her.

In the deep gray dimness, Max locates a wall of flashlights. She selects a small one for Sabine and a bulky square one for herself. With her teeth, she rips open the packages and then loads the lights with batteries swiped from the checkout lane. On the chance that the batteries run out, she grabs some neon glow sticks wrapped in black foil.

Sabine asks, "You gonna pay for that stuff?"

"You bet," Max tells her, sending a shaft of pale light into the dark rafters of the upper levels. "In fact, I'm going to buy the whole store."

She unwraps a Mighty Good Granola Cookie and gives it to Sabine, then opens a second for herself. It tastes like chocolate chalk, but Max devours it just the same. She tosses a handful into the backpack. From the cooler nearby, they each grab a couple bottles of water. Max chugs one greedily and okays Sabine's request for a Sprite.

Armed with the flashlights, they explore the larger store, wandering from aisle to aisle. They find camping supplies—tents and walking sticks, folding chairs and mini gas grills, binoculars. They slosh down a row of nothing but fishing rods and bait, and then enter an open section of cam-ouflage clothing in more varieties than Max knew existed. Not just pants and shirts, but baseball caps, raincoats, even baby clothes. She locates some dry pants for her and the girl, along with sweatshirts and some fisherman boots, black plastic that goes up past their knees. Although she's sure they have dressing rooms, they change right there in the open, back-to-back. Max was beginning to forget what it felt like to not be soaking wet.

Next, Max and Sabine come across a display of kayaks and paddles, and Max thinks about righting the ATV and trying to tow one back to the bridge to search again for Eli. She pictures his body facedown, bobbing along those rocky waves. But Max recognizes the impulse to go look for him as foolhardy. She's on her own with this odd child, and she feels the weight of that responsibility. So when she finds a wall of orange life jackets, she slides Sabine's arms through the openings and straps the belt around her waist. The girl asks, "Are we going back outside?"

"No way," Max says. The rest of what she thinks—that the hurricane is coming to *them*—she keeps to herself. Max selects a life vest where the padding isn't too thick, and she finds it's more comfortable to swing the backpack around to her front now, wear it like a pouch across her belly.

"You look like a pregnant lady," Sabine tells her.

Max shines the light so she sees the kid's face, which is beaming with a smile at her own clever line. Angie must be about to enter her third trimester by now, and surely she knows the baby's gender. Max's mind wanders. Does she have a little brother waiting to be born, or is it a sister? That unborn child is the last bit of her father, the final remnant of the family she once had.

Distracted by such thoughts, Max nearly walks into a steady flow of water cascading from the ceiling. She aims her light up and finds water easing from a white ceiling, maybe a leak in the roof above. Satisfied that they've exhausted the first floor, she doubles back to the camping area and grabs some hand-crank lanterns and two sleeping bags from high shelves. Max finds an end cap of ready-to-eat meals in silvery pouches, the kind that can be heated over a Sterno can, and she stuffs a dozen into the crowded backpack. They walk past the firearms area, heading for the stairs to the second floor. Max scans the glass display case, looking over the pistols and rifles. Everything is locked up, but she imagines smashing the glass and getting her hands on something with a little more stopping power. Still, she's never loaded a weapon, let alone fired one, and here in this place, she can't think of why she'd need to. What good are bullets against a hurricane? Outside, Celeste howls, making the windows shiver.

Sabine darts up the stairs ahead of Max, who almost tells her to slow down but then decides against it. After all, alone in an empty building, what real trouble could the kid find? This question is fresh in Max's mind when she hears Sabine scream from above, a sound that sends her sprinting up the steps into the darkness. The kid's flashlight illuminates the face of a gray wolf, low to the ground and poised to pounce. Its lips curl back in a snarl, fangs exposed, eyes locked open.

Without thought, Max flings her flashlight, and it bonks off the wolf's head and drops to the carpeted floor. The wolf remains unchanged. It doesn't even blink.

"Stuffed," Max declares. She catches her breath and retrieves her flashlight. When she sees Sabine staring at the wolf, trembling still, she kneels down next to her. "It's dead. It can't hurt us. Think of it like a big stuffed animal."

Sabine twists Jasper's face around in her arm and grimaces, and Max regrets the comparison. She's coming to the conclusion that she's not so good at this big-sister thing.

All around them, the wind whistles and whines, battering the boards nailed tight over the handful of windows. Max aims her light behind the wolf, where a raccoon stands in the shadow of a black bear up on its hind legs, reaching up to twelve feet with its massive claws. Past the bear is a buck with an impressive rack of pointy antlers, bending as if to drink from a stream. There's also a snarling boar like the ones that chased her and Eli this afternoon, along with a mountain lion standing on a fake rock and a bright red fox posed over a stuffed pheasant.

Max sees a strange shine in the girl's eyes. She tells her, "None of them can hurt you. They're all dead. Really."

But Sabine doesn't seem comforted. She wraps one arm around Max's leg. Max hesitates, then settles a hand on the girl's shoulder, using the other to shine her light across a whole pantheon of stuffed heads mounted on the wall: a half-dozen deer, two rams, a moose, another bear, and something that must be an antelope of some sort. Max can feel something unsettle in her, like those dead beasts are judging her. Once, these eyes saw the world. Once, blood pumped through these creatures' veins. There was a day when each awoke and went out into the world—the forest or the swamp or the prairie—unsuspecting and doomed. And now, though lifeless, these animals seem to gaze on Max. She feels as though she is intruding in the land of the dead.

Sabine seems to hear these thoughts, and she speaks in a voice Max recognizes as a version of Mother Evangeline's: "The dead are all around us. They don't never really go."

Rather than try to argue, Max moves her light away from the heads, letting the dead return to shadow. They find an open entryway with the words OBSERVATION PLATFORM: NO MERCHANDISE! on a sign above the door. Max realizes this must be the central tower, where they will be highest when this storm surge thing comes, and she leads Sabine inside. They begin to climb the spiral stairs, but then a sound makes them pause, something like the rippling of creek water. The wind gets louder, and when they reach the top, Max is met with a staggering sight: a huge chunk of roof has collapsed, and the open sky above them pours in wind and rain. This, she knows, must be the source of the weeping ceiling downstairs.

Without comment, she turns and leads Sabine back down to the second floor. Far from the crumbling central tower, in a corner away from the stuffed creatures, Max locates an open area by a display for a deer stand, where they roll out their sleeping bags. Sabine looks back toward the menagerie, and Max says, "Come lie down." Obediently, Sabine sits on the floor. She tilts her red helmet to make a nest for Jasper. Max works the hand crank on a lantern, casting an eerie illumination on the hunting books and fishing guides lining the wall. Max finds a book about birds of Africa and gives it to Sabine for distraction, but it quickly becomes clear that Sabine isn't interested in any book. The kid's just looking at the walls, likely wondering same as Max how long they will hold.

Max digs one of the glow sticks from the backpack. After tearing the thick foil, she cracks the green wand and shakes it, causing the stick to shine with a radiant glow. Sabine takes it and smiles in wonder. "How's it do that?"

Max knows it's some kind of chemical process, but instead, she says, "Magic."

The girl grins, and Max holds up a silvery pouch of Chicken Burrito Bombshell. "You want some more food or something?"

The child tells her no, and Max feels an odd sensation, the gratification of being needed. Sabine is relying on her in a way no one else ever has.

The water on the first floor is rising steadily, and the roof of the tower will likely collapse further. Max can't help but imagine what might happen to this building as the storm gets stronger. She wonders if she should turn the lights out, if maybe they should rest. Would it be better if they were asleep when death came? Would they wake before they died?

Sabine shuffles next to her, sets down the glow stick. "Shouldn't we ought to pray?"

Max looks at the girl's face, smiling hopefully in the greenish glow. "Pray if you want. See if you can get God to shut this storm off."

She regrets her tone, worried that she may have come across as mocking, and she reaches over awkwardly to pat Sabine on the arm. The girl slides over and sets her head on Max's lap, using it like a pillow. Softly, Max brushes a hand over her hair, stroking it gently.

Max sees the girl's lips twitching with prayer. If she were the praying type, what would she pray for? Would she ask to be back in Jersey, out of harm's way? Would she want to go back in time and say a proper good-bye to her father? Maybe she'd erase how she acted when Angie came around and try to be more accepting. Her mind free-floats through all these impossibilities. But one wish keeps returning, insistent. It seems too much to ask to have him restored to them, but she'd give anything just to know: What happened to Eli?

Chapter Nine

I'M SPINNING IN A STORM OF BLACKNESS AND WIND, FLIPPING around and upside down with no sense of whether I'm rising or falling. Blood rushes to my head, and it's hard to suck in a good breath. At first, I stretch my arms way out, but then I cross them over my face and try to curl up my body, waiting on the crash that's got to be coming. I'm hoping for water but picturing the iron girders of the bridge. But I don't crash at all. Something whacks the back of my head—hard enough that I taste blood—but somehow I don't die. Lightning crackles from the tumbling clouds, and I just keep on twirling away, time stretching out all dizzy, like in a dream.

But this is a dream like no other. Little by little, my spinning starts to slowly settle, sort of like the end of a wild amusement ride, and when it stops, I'm flying still. The rain is gone, and the storm has calmed. Craziest thing of all, though— even crazier than me floating like a kite—is that all the color's been drained from the world. Below me is a sketched version of the iron bridge, etched in perfect pencil. It's like I'm alive in some 3-D version of my black-and-white drawings.

And I'm gliding now over the intercostal waters, shaded in dusty gray swirls, and the water tower at the edge of town. I drift away from town, and before I know it, I'm passing above the shingled roof of my home and the Chenier Sanctuary. None of this makes sense, but I have the strange feeling that I'm controlling my flight through power of will. Next I'm hovering high above the houses by the Chains and then, sure enough, Lucy. Like in my sketches, the lighthouse looks strong and certain. I feel the urge to go to it, and my body descends, smooth and gentle as if I were a heron easing down into a cypress tree.

Waiting on the crow's nest is a single figure, one I know long before I can see her face. Celeste is etched in grays and blacks, standing at the rail, gazing over a calm ocean. My feet touch down softly behind her, and above us both a thousand stars dot the clear summer sky. Years of my prayers have been answered at last, and I'm back at the night of my greatest failure. I've been given a second chance.

"Stop!" I shout.

My sister turns to me. "You shouldn't be here," she says. "Go on home."

These lines are pulled from the script in my mind, the one that draws right from my memory. We said these same things the last time I saw her. "We should go home together. I know you're sad, Celeste, but I need you."

"You don't need me, kiddo. You, you're great. You've got it all covered. Just quit worrying about everything so much."

I want to tell her how things will change after this night if she does what she's about to do, how sad Mom and Dad will get, how alone I'll be in a world without her. But I'm not in control of my body at all. I'm trapped in the memory of what was, chained to the past. "I love you," I say, just the same as I said before.

"I feel your love. And it's all that's kept me here for this long. Don't you understand? You're the brightest spot in my life, but I need more than that. You belong here, Eli. And me, I just don't." Her eyes are glassy and steady, sad but determined. She slides up onto the crow's nest rail, legs dangling, facing me still. "Okay, then," she says, and her hands come away from the railing. As she crosses her arms over her chest, I remember what she's about to do. At the time, the realization struck like lightning. Maybe the shock of it froze me. But in my dreamy state, just like when it really happened, I do nothing. I don't charge forward and grab her, tackle her. I don't scream "no." I stand there like a hunk of nothing, and I watch my sister lift her legs and tilt over backward, and then there's just open space and the ocean where she'd been. I rush into the rail, and just like before, I see her tumbling in slow motion toward the rocks.

In moments, after I race down the lighthouse stairs, I'll be at her side, and the blood will be awful, and her crooked limbs will be awful, and she'll beg me to stay with her—*Just stay, Eli! Don't you leave me!*—but leave her is exactly what I'll do. I'll run for help and try to drive her red pickup truck and crash into an oak tree a half mile up the road, and she will die and I'll be alone, a useless screwup. And one day, I'll end up back in that same lighthouse myself.

I can't stand to relive those scenes again, and so, while my sister is still falling in the dream, I break free from the script of what was. I leap over the railing myself and sweep down after her, sleek as a hawk. I'll catch up to her and stretch out my arms, latch on to her shoulders, and fly us both to safety. I'll be the hero and save Celeste.

Only as I'm falling, suddenly I can't control my flying. I find myself starting to tumble and spin, and before I know it, I'm twirling wild. I lose sight of my sister and the rocks below the lighthouse, and instead, all I can see is blackness mixed with flashing light. Raining hard as it is, it's not easy to tell when the water stops and the air starts. Somehow, I splash into cold waves, and the impact shocks my eyes shut. My body gets tossed up and down as I struggle to stay above the surface. I catch a glimpse of metal webwork on a piece of land not far off. Gasping, I swim toward solid ground, kicking and stretching with my aching arms.

I don't so much reach land as get heaved onto it by the waves, dumped into a bed of reedy grass, but I'm quick to stumble to my feet and stagger away from the water. In the mud and muck, I lean into one of the bridge's support beams, dropping down so I'm sitting on the concrete base. I breathe and try to settle myself, taking stock of what just happened. I reach around to the back of my head, where something thwacked me in midair, and I find a good-sized goose egg. Was that black-and-white vision a weird dream, some sort of holy hallucination?

My confusion only gets worse when I finally lift my head to look around. The landscape's all wrong, no houses or docks like there ought to be. And it's then I realize that the hurricane didn't blow me back to the island. It blew me to the mainland, on the far side of the bridge.

Like a jolt of electricity, all the weariness in my mind and aches in my body sizzle out. I high-step through the weedy grass, to where the water's up almost to the road. I run to the drawbridge control booth where Dallas used to spend his hot summer days, but when I grab the knob and tug, nothing happens. It's locked up tight. I can see the controls that'll lower the bridge and let Max and Sabine get to safety. All that's keeping me from them is a pane of glass, one of those with a metal net crisscrossed inside.

I scramble around in the pouring rain, looking for a brick or a rock, but there's nothing along either side of the road, nor under the bridge. I return to the booth and pound on the reinforced glass, peel off one boot and beat on it, all just wasted effort.

Finally, I see the lowered crossing arm, the long board with a big stop sign nailed to the middle of it. It's wobbling like mad in the wind. I run over and grab the free end. When I start walking it backward, the long board bends easily at first, curving like a bow. After a few feet, it begins to offer some resistance, and I need to bear down, dig in my feet, and really shove. I lean so hard I'm practically sideways, shouldering now into the board as I gain another foot. The board strains, and I imagine it springing straight, snapping back and launching me like an arrow. Instead, there's a mighty splintering sound, and I collapse forward, right on top of a six-foot section.

I grab the wood with both hands, charge at the booth, and drive my battering ram into the glass. The wood slides in my grip, and the window is untouched. I back up and try it again, and this time a slim crack appears, forking like lightning. I take a batter's stance and pound away, and only after I hear myself roaring into the storm do I realize I'm yelling. But even this doesn't do much good. The metal net inside the window keeps it from shattering, so I end up with a battered and cracked barrier, but a barrier all the same. Frustrated, I drive my fist into the window, spiking pain into my knuckles. I shake my hand out and open it up. The palm is scratched with splinters from the board, and the skin's all scraped up from climbing the bridge, gripping hard the rusty iron.

That thought sends me to the rail work, dragging my wooden board behind me. I lift it up again like a six-foot base-ball bat, eyeing up the X shape of some of those crossed pistols. I swing that sucker and connect good, and lo and behold, for once my plan actually works. There on the wet ground is my prize. I drop the board and reach for the crossed pistols. The metal is cool and rough in my hand, and the edges are jagged blades.

Back at the booth, with my improvised weapon tight inside my fist, I punch the reinforced glass, driving some pieces right through that metal net. I punch again, ignoring the biting sting in my palm, and again, picturing Max and Sabine on the far side waiting. Must be I get lost in my thoughts, 'cause even after I break through, I keep swinging at the pieces around the edges, smashing all I can smash.

Huffing with effort, I drop the metal X and shove my hand inside, stretching for the doorknob's lock. I catch some shards and shred up my wrist a bit, but it's not enough to worry over now. I feel for the latch with my fingers and flip it, and when I grab the door, it swings open, and at last, I'm inside.

It's just like I remembered, the two safety switches and the large lever, the key, even the old barstool where Dallas used to sit. But the safety switch isn't glowing red like it's supposed to be when the bridge is up. And it's not green either. The light is dull and dead, and I realize now there's nothing lit up on the control panel. Hoping maybe I don't remember right, I reach for the key, pinch it, and turn. The dull buttons don't ignite. The damn booth's got no power.

I grab the lever with both hands and yank down, then shove it up and yank down again and again, pumping it to the point where I wouldn't be surprised if it snapped clean off. The bridge doesn't notice my rage. The raised section stays raised, and I slide down onto the floor with the broken glass, feeling pretty busted up myself.

I try to think clearly for a second, consider my options. On any normal day, the walk from where I am to Hackberry along Highway 27 would take about an hour. In these conditions, I think it'd be at least double that, probably more. The terrain is open and flat, nothing but a few fishing shacks off in the marsh. If I'm out there when the storm surge hits, the rushing floodwaters will sweep me away. That's saying nothing about the winds, which soon enough will be on the wrong side of a hundred miles per hour. But if I'm wanting to live through this, it's head up Highway 27 or try to climb back over that damn bridge. I couldn't make it across the bridge when I had more of my strength and hadn't been half drowned. I look at my right hand, bruised and busted up, pulsing with pain and slick with blood. Forming a loose fist makes me wince.

Sitting on the floor of that booth, though, I think again of Max and Sabine. I imagine them on the other side of the iron bridge, looking up at the raised section, waiting for it to lower and make clear their way. They need me. I picture myself walking north, alone and without purpose. Eli the Screwup— same as I ever was, same as I'll ever be. The emptiness that drove me to the lighthouse this morning begins to expand in my gut.

Celeste's ghost doesn't appear, but in my head her voice echoes: *Give it up. You can't do anything right.* Plenty of times, I've felt that way myself. And I know it's how everybody thinks of me. But I don't want to be that guy anymore. The climb back over is impossible, epic. The kind of thing that could only be made by a guy way better than me.

In the booth, I rise up off the floor and turn to the iron bridge.

Chapter Ten

MAX IS BACK IN JERSEY ON THE BEACH, DOWN AT AVON-BY-the-Sea where she and her dad fixed up a half-dozen seaside homes and helped restore a dilapidated merry-go-round. Even though the sun is hot, baking the sand, she's carrying her flip-flops and walking along the water's cool edge. Alongside her, away from the ocean, Angie strolls along, wearing an oversized sun hat and slick sunglasses. But on Max's other side, there's a toddler, a little girl unsteady on her feet in the squishy sand. Max needs to hold her hand to keep her upright. The tide slips up and rushes over their bare feet, and the child squeals with wonder and delight. Max thinks of all the things she could show her.

"You should wake up."

Max opens her eyes. She's on the second floor of the Sportsman's Castle, and Sabine is leaning over her, pushing on her shoulder. "What were you smiling about?"

"Just a stupid dream. What's wrong?"

"You have to wake up. Something's downstairs."

Max rubs her neck. She can't tell if she was asleep for fifteen minutes or two hours. "Something like what?"

"Like I don't know. A something. I heard it knocking around."

Max regards the girl. The hurricane's roaring creates a constant backdrop, a low-grade growl, loud enough that they have to raise their voices. So she's not sure how the kid could hear anything downstairs. "It's just your imagination," she tells her.

Sabine looks hurt by this. She says, "You was dreaming about a baby girl. Your sister, I think."

Max blushes. "How'd you know that?"

"Sometimes I go walking in other people's dreams. Mother Evangeline, she taught me."

"Yeah, right," Max says, unsure how to respond.

The girl shrugs, holds on to her stuffed animal. "Jasper's real afraid of what's downstairs."

Max reaches for the big flashlight. She says, "Well, I'm real afraid of what's outside. But I sure wouldn't want Jasper to be upset. You tell him I'm on the case."

Just to placate the kid, Max crawls off the sleeping bag and clicks on the flashlight. Cautiously, she prowls through the taxidermist's graveyard. At the second-floor railing, she shines the beam downstairs. Instantly, she can see things have gotten a lot worse. The floodwaters have risen up a couple feet, and the first floor has become a gently sloshing sea with merchandise floating and rocking on the surface. Boxes bump and tumble into each other, and this is surely the noise that bothered the kid. Max sees a corpse dressed all in camouflage, floating facedown, but then realizes she's looking at a toppled mannequin. Even though she knows it's not real, Max doesn't want to settle on this image, as it makes her think of where the two of them might be in a few hours. Will their bodies even be found?

This thought makes her turn from the mannequin, and she aims the light away from the dummy. It lands by chance on a display that catches Max's immediate interest. On a big sign, a cartoon hunter proclaims PICKS UP A WHISPER FIVE MILES AWAY! He's holding some sort of walkie-talkie.

Max doubts that outside the Odenkirks' there's any living soul within five miles of her, let alone one who might be tuning in to obscure radio frequencies. But maybe the Coast Guard or emergency services are scanning the channels. As she moves toward the stairs, she thinks of that clichéd expression that seems to have defined her life lately: Nothing to lose.

As she reaches the bottom steps, she wades into the water without much worry, so used is she to being damp and wet. It rises halfway up her thighs, which stay dry in the tall fishermen's boots. She plows past two aisles to the walkie-talkie display. The "Hunters' Helper" is guaranteed to broadcast in any terrain, even where cell phone service isn't available. It works on some sort of CB radio technology, and according to a red, white, and blue sticker, it's "Made Right Here in the Heartland of the U.S. of A.!" Much more important, she finally locates the information she does need: It takes a single nine-volt battery.

With heavy strides, she shoves her way through the floating debris to the checkout lanes. She locates the batteries and loads up the walkie-talkie, not feeling guilty in the least about dropping the packaging into the water.

When she flips on the walkie-talkie, it crackles with static. Even that sound excites her. She turns a knob, and a red digital counter slips from 1 up to 19—channels, she assumes. Max extends the antennae, then goes back through the channels slowly, listening to the static coming from each. Here and there she imagines a voice breaking through the chattering crackle, someone saying, "You're not alone." On each setting, only after she's sure she can't hear anything, she thumbs the button on the side and cradles the receiver, yelling, "Hello! We're here! My name is Max, and me and a little girl are stranded in the Sportsman's Castle on Shackles Island. The water is getting higher. We're trapped, and we need help now!"

"Jasper too!" Sabine hollers from where she's watching above at the rail.

Max wonders what else a listener would need to hear. "This isn't a joke or a prank. We're in real trouble out here. Mayday! SOS! The Sportsman's Castle on Shackles Island. Please help us!" At every channel, after sending her message, she again grips the walkie-talkie and strains her hearing, tuning hard to the static, waiting for some voice to emerge, some slim hope of rescue.

On the last channel, she refuses to turn it off without an answer. She closes her eyes and concentrates until she's convinced she hears the faint tinkle of piano music. But this can only be her dreaming.

Angry and scared, she heaves the walkie-talkie across the checkout lanes, where it plunks into the murky water. Right after it lands, though, it somehow burbles back to the surface. There's some disturbance there in the gently sloshing waves. Max wades through the drifting junkyard of gum and candy bars and *Hunter's World!* magazines to shine the flashlight in the area where the walkie-talkie landed. And then the light catches on two shiny black marbles about ten feet away, rising just above the waterline.

Above her, Sabine yells, "Ivory!"

Max sees Sabine standing at the railing on the second floor, horrified, pointing to where the eyes had been. When Max looks again, they're gone.

Driven by instinct, she swings up onto a checkout counter, clearing her feet from the murk just as Ivory's snapping jaws rise after her. The albino alligator chomps air, collapses back into the water, and lifts again instantly, clawing now at the metal sides of the checkout lane. Max backs away, her slick boots nearly slipping on the rubbery conveyor belt. Ivory thrashes in the water, churning it, trying to get high enough to climb onto the countertop. More than once, his massive head makes it up, but the weight of his body pulls him back down.

Max scans the water surrounding her. It's thirty feet to the stairs, way too far to make a break for it—and what's to say this monster can't climb steps? She'd just be leading it to Sabine. Ivory launches once more from below, and Max sees the rows of yellowed teeth in his mouth. Without thinking, she leaps across the open space between checkout lanes and lands on the next countertop over. It's far from a perfect landing—it takes wild arm-swinging to maintain her balance—and she nearly slips on the rubber soles of the boots. She tugs them off, certain that if she needs to make such a leap again, she'd be better off barefoot.

Ivory swims around and begins circling Max's new perch. After a few loops, he settles down beneath her, hanging just below the surface with only his eyes exposed. In the dim light, his scaly skin seems more pink than white. Max uses her flashlight to confirm that the row of checkout lanes ends far short of the steps. Some shelves would take her higher up, but getting to them means going into the water, and that's the worst idea ever. She scans the area for some kind of weapon, but there's nothing. Desperate, she squats over the register and grabs hold of both sides. She heaves it up and waddles carefully to the edge of the counter, holding it just over the space where Ivory had been. But he's retreated a few feet, clearly out of range. He's watching her again, and their eyes come together. Max remembers what Eli said, how the alligators were so patient, they didn't mind waiting for prey to rot. Maybe somewhere in his reptilian brain, Ivory knows what Max does, that the floodwaters are rising.

With this thought, Max heaves the cash register as far as she can. It crashes into the water with a cannonball splash, a few feet short of Ivory. And after the water calms, she can see him exactly where he was before the attack, waiting for the inevitable.

Chapter Eleven

I SWEAR THAT THE SECOND MY FEET MAKE CONTACT WITH the solid ground of Shackles Island, some energy sparks from the rain-slicked roadway up through my boots and legs. If anybody were here to witness my success, I imagine them clapping. Sure, I'm Eli LeJeune, lost cause and loser, the kid who couldn't save his big sister. But I also just crossed a raised drawbridge in a hurricane, a climb I had no right making. And for the moment, despite everything this storm's throwing my way, I'm alive. That's got to count for something.

The trip back over was all I expected it'd be. I wasn't even twenty feet in when my grip gave way and my feet slipped. But somehow I held on, too stubborn to die, I guess. After that, I stopped worrying and just fell into a zone. I'd reach and grab and pull, shift my boots, reach and grab again. I didn't let the idea of slipping or falling enter into my mind, and go figure, I didn't. Maybe there's some kind of big lesson in there, but this isn't the time to dwell on it. Somewhere ahead of me, Max and Sabine are trying to ride out the storm, and somehow I need to find them.

The gulf has nearly claimed the whole island, from beach to intercostal, and we still got the storm surge coming. If Max had to find shelter, where would she take the kid? I look at the nearest houses along the intercostal. Too close to the water's edge. She wouldn't be that dumb. And no way she'd go back to the Odenkirks'. No, Max would head for higher ground. Course there's not but a handful of buildings that even begin to qualify, being more than one story. Most of them are in town, mostly up on Infinity Road, so I lean into the wind and start dragging my heavy legs through the rushing water, which only grows deeper.

Right now, I bet my mom and dad are watching the Weather Channel, wondering where I am. I'm sure the TV's showing pictures of some correspondent up in Lake Charles or over in Beaumont, no doubt in some dark hotel parking lot wearing a raincoat and getting blown sideways by the rain and wind. They always drop the same kind of tired line: "I pity anyone who's caught out in this." My mom's sitting on my aunt's couch in Galveston, clutching my dad's arm. And he pats her hand and leans in close to say, "I'm sure he got out. Eli's in a shelter somewhere far from the coast."

For the life of me, I can't remember why I didn't call her when I had the chance. She doesn't deserve this.

Those thoughts that floated through my head before about my parents not caring if I never came back . . . I see them now as part of a screwed-up mind-set I get wrapped up in sometimes. I know they love me. I know they don't blame me for what happened with Celeste, at least not directly. Same as me, they got rattled by her death, and afterward, nothing was the same for any of us. It's like we were survivors of some natural disaster, left wondering why we're still alive when everything around us got destroyed. When you're faced with destruction on a massive scale, it's hard to find a good reason to give a damn about anything. Everybody deals with that their own way, and mine I guess was to curl up inside myself, be like a turtle tucked inside its shell. If I somehow live through all this and see them again, maybe we'll find some way to really talk about me and Celeste and the lighthouse and all that's happened since.

When I finally reach the town's main intersection, all the buildings I can see through the slashing rain—the police station and the library and Zeb's Gas 'n' Geaux—are darkened and boarded up. The courthouse is sturdy and a couple stories. But just beyond the edge of my vision, I can imagine the tall spire of the Sportsman's Castle to the east, nearly at the end of the island. Max mentioned that place earlier, and it'd be as good a place as any to ride out the storm. It's a long shot, but I head in that direction, crossing Zeb's parking lot. Something big and bulky floats my way, and at first, I think it's the hump of a garfish, but it's just a garbage can on its side getting dragged along by the current.

The gas sign has been stripped clear of any numbers, so you can only guess the price for regular, premium, or diesel. The whole thing rocks back and forth so much so I don't know how it hasn't snapped. Just past it, the phone pole leans and sways even worse, way more than I'd think it could without breaking. Almost like it's heard my thoughts, the wind rises into what sounds like a freight train bearing down on me, so loud I clap my hands over my ears. With a thunderous snap, the phone pole fractures halfway up, ripping wires loose as it drops down onto Zeb's roof. There's a hell of a crash. I look back to the open space where the phone pole used to be, and that's when I see what's really making that freight-car scream.

The funnel of swirling debris is a hundred feet tall and twisting, spinning, whipping like a thing alive. Hurricane Celeste has given birth to a tornado.

The tornado's winds reach inside Zeb's and start looting. The air around me swarms with a flock of magazines. Candy bars and beer cans rocket through the air, shattered glass and bricks, all of it shrapnel. I cross my arms over my face and hightail it for a Dumpster in the back corner of the parking lot. This means I need to charge into the flying crap. Something punches me in the gut, and a quick slice burns across my neck. Luckily, that Dumpster lid's already opened, so I just heave myself up and drop down into a swampy bed of soaked trash bags. The rotten stink's enough to make me gag as I slam the lid behind me. The debris from Zeb's does a chaotic drum solo on the metal walls of my shelter, banging away like mad. Celeste seems pissed indeed. She tries to yank the Dumpster lid free, but at the first rattle, I grab hold with both hands, anchoring it good. There's a frustrated cry, loud enough to deafen me, and more pounding against the Dumpster's hull.

I'm sure it's not more than a minute or so till that tornado passes, but it feels a lot longer. My aching biceps are grateful when the pressure on the lid eases up. Once I'm sure it's over,

I push into the plastic top and emerge like some submarine commander. My Dumpster's been shoved twenty feet or so into the middle of the parking lot. Where Zeb's used to be, there's just a single brick wall remaining, one with a freezer backed up against it. Scattered junk and debris drifts on the floodwaters. It looks like a bomb went off.

I lower myself back down into the trash and let the lid close behind me. I've got to gather my wits. That tornado nearly took me out. Dying's a funny thing when you think you're facing it on your own terms, when it's your idea and you control it. But when it's some outside force trying to kill you, you can't help but want to fight against it. Some part of me is glad for the struggle, and it feels good to want to live. If I ever see the Odenkirks again, maybe I ought to thank them.

Something shifts beneath me in the trash, down under the plastic bags. Something alive and skittering. I scramble over the bags crab-style, kicking in the direction of the movement. The sound that comes back is a hiss and a bitter meow, and I realize one of the island's stray cats was smart enough to find its way into the Dumpster. I must have spooked it good before, when I invaded its hiding place. "S'okay," I say into the darkness, and I kiss the air a few times. To my surprise, I feel a light pressure on my legs, and something works its way up to my lap. My fingers find fur, knotted and sticky with grime. But even so, when I scratch a bit, the cat bumps its head into my hand. It does a few circles on my lap and drops down, and I can feel it purring, like a little humming engine. The stench coming off the cat is a mix of sewer and old tuna.

"Well, Stinky, at least we got each other," I say, and I instantly hear how crazed I sound. But still, it does give me comfort, having something else here with me. That was another one of Father Arceneaux's lines, that he knew I felt alone but I wasn't. He told me some sappy story about a lady walking on a beach with Jesus, something about footprints in the sand.

Even before what happened with Celeste, I never was one much for deep devotion and prayer, but I know at times like this, the faithful find comfort by asking God for help. If I had any right, I might make such a request. Petting this cat in the pitch black, I try to think what prayer I might offer, which recited words would be right for this situation. What's strange is that as my mind roams through the things it wants most, I find myself picturing Max and Sabine. Actually finding them is a pipe dream, but I wonder if through some miracle they found someplace safe. It seems too much to ask for the storm to stop or pass us by, but I just wish I knew. I wish I had one of those signs Father Arceneaux told me were all around, just waiting to be noticed.

These are the thoughts I'm having when I hear the bell. At first, I'm certain it's my imagination, drumming up the sound from my desire. But even Stinky stirs on my lap, and I say, "You hear that too?"

St. Jude's has got to be ten blocks west, and with the wind howling like it is, it doesn't make sense that the sound could get to us here. Yet when I lift the Dumpster lid and listen, the gonging I'd heard before is even louder. And it doesn't seem random to me, like the clanging of a buoy tossed on rocky waves. It's rhythmic and clear. High up in the steeple, some-body's ringing that bell, like just before mass, when they sum-mon all the true believers.

I climb out of the Dumpster and hop back down into the black, streaming water. Stinky comes right up to the metal lip, ignoring the dowsing rain and eyeballing me good. "You'll be safer in here," I tell her, and I try to decide if I should lower the lid or not. Either way her odds aren't real good. But even when I bring the lid down close to her head, she doesn't back down. "Go on," I say. "Git!"

In response, she springs forward, launching herself at me with claws outstretched. I catch her as she hits my chest, and I decide maybe Stinky isn't the right name. Maybe I should go with Crazy. Yeah, well, come join the club.

Cradling that cat like a child, with her head tucked high on my shoulder, I start slogging west through the rushing floodwaters. The wind spits rain in my face so hard I dip my chin to my chest, not even looking where I'm going. Like back on the iron bridge, I focus on just moving one foot, then the next.

Celeste would've loved this storm. She was always a wild child, and when the summer thunderstorms blew in, she'd go down to the beach to meet them. She always wanted to be out hiking along the waterways in the marsh, beachcombing along the shore, bushwhacking through the forest. She loved Fort Abeniacar and the lighthouse. All she used to read were history books, not dumb novels full of fake love and romance. She read about the Aztecs and Mayans, once-mighty civilizations that disappeared without a trace. Sometimes at night, she'd read me her favorite pages.

One time we were alone at the lighthouse, about a month before the end, and she was smoking one of her cigarettes and gazing out on the ocean for a long while. This was just after she got suspended from school for about the fiftieth time. Dad had let loose again with the lecture number 7, the one about living under his roof, abiding by his rules, and we'd escaped again to the lighthouse. Up in the crow's nest, I saw that Celeste had begun to sniffle back tears, and she was never one for crying. I couldn't help but ask her what was wrong. She swiped her cheeks and said, "Just everything. I love you, Eli, but other than you, there's nothing right with my life. I don't think I was supposed to be born here, in this place and time."

I thought before I asked, "Well then, when were you supposed to be born?"

She shook her head. "A long time ago, I think . . . I try to get along here. So help me, I do. But I'll never fit in. My whole life, I'll be a stranger."

I knew my sister was sad. I knew she had problems. But till that last night at the lighthouse, I swear I didn't understand how serious they were. I know now that I should have, that I had the chance to set things right and save her. I know I failed her, and there's no way I can ever go back and right that wrong. Just got to live with my mistake, try to make up for it. Wait for a chance to get it right.

This makes me remember something Father Arceneaux said once in a sermon: "There can be no absolution without penance." He said those words right in the church I'm coming up on. St. Jude's is a brick building without much ornamentation, just some slim stained-glass windows along the sides, though just now thick plywood protects them. A white steeple caps the slanted roof, and indeed, that bell is clanging away pretty good. "We're here," I tell Stinky, and I carry her up the stone steps out of the water. But when I grip the golden doorknob and tug, nothing happens. I try the other door, and it too is locked tight. With my free hand I bang on the door. "I'm here!" I yell. "Max! Sabine! I heard the bell, and I came!"

Undisturbed, the bell just keeps on ringing. I circle the building once, looking for some other sign of entry or a way to break in, but there's nothing. No sign of Charity's ATV either. Back out front, I stand before the statue of St. Jude, arms outstretched, set in an alcove about four feet off the ground. He doesn't seem especially concerned about the storm. I lift Stinky up next to him and then hoist myself beside her. Together we crawl our way into the space behind the statue, which gives us a little cover from the wind and the rain. At the feet of the patron saint of lost causes, I huddle up with a stray cat and wonder how long I'll have, if I've done enough penance, or if not, just how much more I need to do.

The wind dies down for a quick spell, just long enough for the bell to settle into silence. The sound nearly drives me to tears.

Too exhausted to move and too anxious to sleep, for a long while I just watch the floodwaters slowly rise. Before long, they've swallowed most of the church bulletin board and its message: "GOD BE WITH US ALL IN THE STORM." The few cars on the street, abandoned in the rush to evacuate, have water up past their bumpers, and sometime soon, they'll start to float. The surface of the water bubbles with all kinds of crap—busted-up wood and garbage and whatever folks left behind. At one point, a beach ball floats by, rainbow-colored and inflated to near bursting. It bounces along the waves like it was getting tossed by kids at the beach, moving inland with the flow of the water. I lean out to watch it disappear, and in the far-off darkness, two shining eyes greet me.

The headlights—for sure and for certain that's what they are—are distant, maybe a quarter mile off. At first, I'm not even sure they're moving, but gradually they get larger, and above the wind I can hear a truck engine rattle. When the truck is just a block off, I can see it plowing through the flood, churning the water with its monstrous wheels. I scoot down from my post, grab Stinky, and wade out into the middle of the street, waving one hand like I'm flagging down a passing boat from some desert island beach. The Humvee stops, the engine idling loud, and I charge around to the passenger side, where I've got to step up onto a footrest to pull myself out of the water. I swing the door back and slide onto the seat, out of the rain.

Gripping the steering wheel, Sweeney says, "Hey, you found a cat." Stinky crawls over to his lap, and his hand drops down and strokes her automatically. "Just what in the hell are you doing out here?"

"Waiting to drown," I say. "How about yourself? Weren't you headed to Lake Charles?"

"I been there before," he says. "I pulled the bullet out of that deer, and it weren't but a .22. Standard issue, nothing the shadow-government types would use. Funny how your head can play tricks with you." He looks at me here like I'm supposed to say something, but I don't, and he goes on, "Anyway, I figured I'd ride this one out. My place is high and dry. All my improvements and renovations running five by five."

"That's good," I say. "So you just out for a joyride now, enjoying the weather?"

He taps a walkie-talkie on the dashboard. "Caught a message from somebody who claims to be on the island still, in rough shape. Figured I'm gonna mount me a rescue operation. No chance you know some girl name of Max, huh?"

Chapter Twelve

INSIDE THE SPORTSMAN'S CASTLE, THE WATER HAS RISEN TO within half a foot of the checkout counter where Max perches. She can't figure out why Ivory hasn't lurched up and attacked, instead of just drifting in the waves a few feet away, watching her with those lifeless eyes, patient as death itself. Above her and across the store, Sabine stands at the railing of the second floor. She yells, "What you want I should try next?"

Already, at Max's direction, the girl has heaved dozens of items down for her: hunting knives, coils of rope, even some walking sticks that Max thought might make a decent weapon. But the distance is too far, and Sabine's arm isn't nearly strong enough. The knives plopped like rocks down into the water, but the sticks and the ropes bob along the surface, joining all the other merchandise that's been liberated from the lower shelves. But anything of value, anything that might help her escape her predicament, remains tantalizingly out of reach. Max cups both hands to her mouth and hollers over the wind, "Just hang on for a minute."

Once more she eyes the kayaks along the far wall and thinks of the guns. She could have the kid try to smash the glass of the display case and load up a rifle for her; probably she's fired a weapon before. But the guns are on the first floor, and that means having Sabine wade in water that'd be way up past her belly, water where Ivory could be in seconds. That isn't an option.

Exhausted, Max kneels down on the checkout counter. She's trying to decide at what point to just make a break for the stairs. Would it be better to go slowly in hopes of not attracting Ivory's attention, or just follow her instincts and run like hell?

A shiny aluminum packet bobs up to the edge of the checkout lane. Max picks it up and strains to read in the dark, but she's able to make out "Beef Stroganoff Supreme." It's one of those ready-to-eat meals in a pouch. More out of curiosity than anything else, Max tears a corner and sniffs. The smell is meaty and pungent, and Max has a hard time imagining eating whatever's inside, which looks wet and raw. With a flip of her wrist, she tosses it Frisbee-style out into the water, without aim or purpose. It sails over Ivory's head and plunks down ten feet past him.

But the moment it enters the water, the gator stirs. He swishes his tail and slides over to investigate, and Max loses sight of him. She squints and locates the metal shine of the pouch, and she's watching when Ivory's jaw flashes open, then submerges. The pouch is gone, and so is Ivory.

"What was that?" Sabine shouts from above.

"I got an idea," Max yells back. Searching the water around her, she's able to gather a half dozen of the pouches: two Beef Stroganoff Supreme, two Swedish Meatball Madness, and two Hamburger Mac-and-Cheese Delight. Once she's ready, she plans on ripping a tear in each one and throwing them through the open space where the ATV smashed through the front door, a gray box of slanted light. If Ivory chases the scent of meat, Max can make a break for the stairs, maybe even do a smash and grab as she bolts past the gun display. The only problem is that, now that she's hatched this escape plan, she can't locate Ivory. She looks up at Sabine. "Can you see him?"

Sabine leans over the railing and turns her head side to side. "It's too dark. Only when he's moving or right up on top."

For a few minutes, both of them watch the water for some sign. The first floor is the size of a small grocery store. That gator could be anywhere, Max thinks. For all she knows, he's wandered off to the aisle where the gourmet meals are and is having his own little feast. What she does know is that the water is just a few inches below the checkout lane now, and it's rising more quickly. One way or the other, she'll be in the murk soon.

Ten minutes later, standing in a thin puddle on the counter, Max decides she can't wait. After taking a deep breath, she tears a rip in one packet, then flings it toward the door, twenty feet away. It lands right at the threshold but comes rushing back inside, driven by the floodwater's current. She watches the pouch, praying for Ivory to snap it up, take the bait. But it just drifts along idly. A minute goes by, then another, and it disappears back into the shadows where she can't see. What does that mean? Has the gator drifted to a far corner of the room? Is his hunger so slight that he's satisfied now?

"Try again!" Sabine yells, watching from her post above.

Though she's not sure what good it will do, Max can't think of a reason not to try, so she cocks back her arm and heaves a second open pouch, putting everything she's got into it. This one flies through the door, out into the parking lot, and Max studies the water at the threshold, hoping to see the pink ridges of the beast's back.

Instead, she's shocked when the figure of a man fills the open space. Some guy stands there in the rain, slender with tan skin, holding the pouch. The stranger asks, "Is this some kind of giveaway?"

Max says, "What?"

The man reaches for the rim of a baseball hat with a fleur-de-lis. "Sweeney Soileau. You call for a taxi?"

Max is trying to make sense of this when she sees something even more astonishing. Eli, unsinkable Eli, pushes past Sweeney, charging into the store and yelling her name.

"I'm here!" she yells back. "Watch out. Stop!"

"Watch out for what?"

She points a finger down. "There's an alligator in here. In the water. The albino one they were keeping in that pen outside."

"Ivory?" Sweeney asks. "I saw him trapped before when

I was on patrol. I busted the lock, reckoned he'd make his way inland. Just wanted to give the old sonuvagun half a chance."

Both men are just inside the door, hip deep in water. Max says, "Well, maybe he'll be grateful for your kindness. But more likely he'll look at you same as he looked at me and try to make you dinner. Your call."

"Ivory's old and harmless," Sweeney says. "Half-blind and lazy from being a tourist attraction. He wouldn't hurt a—"

"Here he comes!" shouts Sabine, pointing.

When Max follows her finger, she can just make out the shape gliding through the water, prehistoric and primal. Ivory eases through the sale displays, passes Max, and slips down the next checkout lane over. He makes a hard right and darts toward Eli and Sweeney.

"C'mon!" Eli shouts. "Back here!"

The men lurch forward in the water, high-stepping, then scramble over the sideways ATV into the closed-off area behind the customer service counter. Ivory slashes behind them, raising his snout up onto the vehicle and snapping at the air. Eli and Sweeney back away until they hit the far corner. Sweeney takes one more step, beyond the edge of the desk, and says, "There's a swing door down here."

At the other end of the counter, Ivory claws at the ATV, trying to mount it. Eli says, "Don't tell him that. See if there's a latch or something."

"Just one of them eye-hook thingamabobs."

"Lock it!" Eli yells. He opens a drawer and throws objects at Ivory: a binder, some scissors, something that might be a stapler. Probably annoyed more than wounded, Ivory retreats and then vanishes again.

Once he's gone, Sweeney removes his hat and wipes a hand through his hair. He looks over at Max and says, "Hey, missy, you might could have a point about him being a bit on the ornery side. I'll give you that."

Max shakes her head and thinks, *This island is full of nothing but winners.* She shouts, "I've been watching the water. It's coming up quicker now than before. I need to make a break for it."

"Stay there!" Sweeney yells. "Movement will attract him for sure."

Eli surveys the water lapping the customer service desk. "Yeah, we got the same situation. I'm surprised he couldn't get over this now if he set his mind to it. This is definitely far from good."

Sweeney holds up the meal pouch, which Max is surprised he didn't drop in the excitement. "What were you doing with this thing?"

"I got him to eat one before. I was trying to trick him into going outside."

"Good plan," Eli says.

"Only in theory," Max responds.

Sweeney scratches the back of his neck. "Yeah, but what next? Say you get him outside. Then you maybe got that ungrateful sumbitch waiting on an ambush? Can't say as I'm a big fan of that."

Max scrunches her face, having not considered this. She asks Sweeney, "Any chance you got a gun?"

"I got a bunch," Sweeney answers. "Just none on my person at the moment. I recognize that presents an unfortunate inconvenience."

From above them, Sabine hollers, "He's over there now!" She points to a space between the customer service counter and the checkout lanes. Ivory seems to be biding his time.

"We got to trap him," Eli says.

"Trap him with what?" Sweeney asks. "Our charm and good looks?"

Eli starts rifling through drawers and cabinets. Max tries to think of some way to help, then holds up the pouches she'd gathered earlier and says, "Hey! You can use that thing he's got as bait."

Eli pauses and glares her way. "Yeah, I got that far on my own. Throw them other ones over."

Max ignores his snarky tone and cocks one arm back, aiming for Eli's head, which she nearly hits. The first pouch slams into the wall and drops in the water. The next one arcs a bit to the right and Eli needs to lean into the ATV to catch it. It's there that he looks down, leans in, and shakes his head. "Unbelievable. God bless them scavenger Odenkirks."

Max isn't sure what he means until she sees him unwinding the rusty chain from the headlight.

"You think he'll try to swallow that?" Max asks.

"I think maybe."

Sweeney extends his arms. "How about you getting him back here behind this little counter? You and me hop over and I close that door, lock him in?"

Eli seems to consider this. He changes places with Sweeney and looks down where Max assumes the swing door must be. "You don't think he'd smash through that cheap wood?"

Sweeney shrugs. "Don't nobody know what a gator's going to do but the gator and God."

"Well, the way I see it—"

"Yo, boys!" Max shouts. "How 'bout you quit comparing testosterone levels and just do both?" When they look her way, equally baffled, she says, "Bait the hook and set it back behind the counter with the door open. If he goes after it, hightail it over the desk and lock him in. Then we'll all make a break for it."

The men nod at each other, and then they get to work. Max, satisfied, glances up at Sabine and tells her, "Grab my backpack and get to the top of the stairs. When I tell you, run down fast as you can and I'll help you through the water. Don't look around at anything. Just run." She's surprised by what she hears in her voice, something more than simple concern or even affection. Is this what it feels like to be a big sister? Is this some version of how Angie feels when she rubs her bulging belly?

The kid flashes a thumbs-up.

"Swedish Meatball?" Eli asks. "Or Mac-and-Cheese Delight?"

"Go with the meatball," Max says.

Eli sinks a hook deep into a pouch and drops it in the water behind the customer service desk. Then he quickly anchors the chain to the ATV. He and Sweeney slide onto the counter, and they wait for ten minutes, all of them in silence as the water rises. Now it's sloshing freely over the checkout counter Max stands on, covering her bare feet. Above them, Sabine reports, "He still ain't moving."

"All right," Eli says. "Time to up the ante."

Sweeney nods. He and Eli rip open the other meal pouches and dip them in the water, letting the meaty juices flow out. Not long after, Sabine yells, "Ivory's gone under! I can't see him no more."

Sweeney, Eli, and Max swivel their heads, their eyes sweeping the surface. Eli checks that the little swing door is open and then backs to the far edge of the countertop. Sweeney makes space for him and says, "This is genuinely ludicrous, yeah?"

"Give it a minute," Eli says. "Then I'll go in the water, head for the far side of the store and draw his attention. You get these two back to your place."

Max yells, "When are you gonna cut that savior crap out? We'll get out of here together."

A great crashing above them turns their heads. The opening in the ceiling where water had been dripping down is now a gaping mouth, with rain pouring through it. Max pictures the collapsed tower.

"I think we got to go," Sweeney announces. "He ain't taking the bait, and we got to get heading to my shelter. That surge, she's due any time now. We'll all move slow." He looks up toward the girl. "Honey child, I'll be coming for you and you climb up on me for a piggyback ride, okay?"

"Jasper's scared. He wants to cry."

Sweeney raises a questioning eyebrow toward Max, who shouts, "Jasper's her teddy bear." She sees that Sabine has the backpack with her father's ashes slung over one shoulder.

"All right, then," Sweeney says. "Jasper can come too. Slow and easy. No splashing or jerky movements."

Sweeney eases into the water on the outside of the desk, and Eli does the same. Max sits on the submerged edge of the checkout counter and then stands in the water, now halfway up her chest. She looks around and whispers, "I'll never say another bad thing about New Jersey."

Fighting the urge to rush, she inches along the lane, then turns toward the door, only thirty feet away. Sweeney is heading for Sabine, still dry on the steps, while Eli makes his way toward the exit with both arms raised high, as if he's surrendering. They share a nervous smile. Eli's right at the end of the desk when he stops cold, staring straight ahead. Max is sure he's spotted Ivory, and her eyes flash to where he's looking.

But it isn't the alligator at all. Against all logic, there in the doorway, leveling a rifle at Eli, stands Judgment Odenkirk. He strides inside, takes in the scene with a smug grin, and says, "Never did get my invitation to this particular reunion. But I'm willing to overlook that breach of etiquette. I reckon this'll do." With both hands, he lifts the gun for effect.

"Who's this now?" Sweeney wants to know. He's got Sabine on his back and is wading toward Eli. As he comes closer to Judge, he says, "I know you. You're Aloysius Odenkirk's boy. I knew your father. He was a good man."

Judge spits in the water. "I knew him to be a drunkard and a liar both. But my momma never gave up on him. I seen you around. That your monster truck out front, yeah?"

Charity appears in the doorway. When she sees the girl, she shouts, "Sabine!"

As Charity charges through the water, Max remembers the alligator. Why wouldn't Ivory have attacked with all this commotion? Maybe he floated out of the store before the Odenkirks arrived, or maybe he's somewhere in the aisles nearby. Max imagines his view, with all these juicy legs ripe for the taking. She shouts, "Look, you guys! We got to get out of here."

But everyone's attention seems focused on Charity, who reaches for Sabine. The girl climbs off Sweeney's shoulders and into her embrace. "Jasper had him some big adventures," she says.

Judge walks closer to the customer service desk. "Sister! Look how they wrecked up your ATV. You all don't handle stolen property very well."

Sweeney advances toward Judge. "Son, you got no cause aiming a weapon at anybody. Come on. You two can come to my place in the sanctuary. It's reinforced good, high and dry. Best spot to weather this storm for sure and for certain."

"There's kids out in our bus," Charity says. "Seven of 'em."

Sweeney says, "That's fine. Might be a bit cramped but we'll make do. Before we can do anything, though, this young man here's got to lower that Remington."

"You're about half right," Judge says. "Here's what we'll do instead. You all can go with Charity to your fancy tree house. Take the rug rats. That's fine, and I'd be in your debt. But me, I need that big truck, yeah. See, my little brothers screwed up good, and my momma's stuck down at the Chains. I got to go fetch them."

"The Chains?" Eli says.

Again, Max says, "Guys, we need to get out of here. Right?"

Eli looks her way, and his eyes slide down to the water. He swallows hard.

Sweeney tilts his head at Judge and says, "Listen good, boy. Anything at the Chains is underwater by now or it's about to be. That storm surge is already past due. I'm sorry about your momma, truly. But I got no intentions of giving you my truck."

"I don't recall asking permission," Judge says, cocking the rifle. "And you left the keys in it." He glances toward Sabine, up in Charity's arms. "I got all I came here for."

Max notices the ATV rocking gently, but she can't tell if it's from the floodwater's ebb and flow or something else under the rippling water.

"Hellfire and hand grenades," Sweeney says. "We ain't got no time for this nonsense. Come on, ya'll, we're getting in my truck. You Odenkirks are welcome to follow us."

Sweeney takes one more step, and the rifle spits a red flash, the gunshot like a shout. Sweeney's body spins, reeling back into Eli's arms. Charity yells, "Judgment!"

Max rushes through the water, but her quick motion draws Judge's attention. He cocks the rifle as he pivots her way. "You and your boyfriend ain't exactly high on my list of popular people right now. I wouldn't be testing my patience."

In Eli's arms, Sweeney says, "Medic? I'm hit." One hand grips the opposite arm, but Max is surprised by how strong his voice sounds. Judge leans back onto the ATV, looking satisfied that he's finally in command. With his rifle resting comfortable across his lap, he says, "Now that we all understand who's got the only vote what matters, let's get on about our business."

"This is crazy," Eli says. "Charity, can't you talk sense into him?"

"I been failing at that for about ten years," she answers.

Sweeney turns his head to say, "You shot me, you hairless moron. I did two tours in Iraq and never got wounded."

"I reckon you'll live. I didn't but wing you."

Suddenly, the ATV shifts. Judge bolts upright, standing clear of the vehicle, and looks back at it. The four-wheeler shimmies in the floodwater, and Max watches the chain attached to the handlebars as it goes loose, then taut. She and Eli lock eyes, and he drags Sweeney a couple steps toward her, away from the desk. Judge says, "What in the hell?" and leans over the ATV to investigate.

When Ivory's jaws explode from the water, they are wide and white with jagged teeth. They latch on to Judge's skull and yank his body forward, folding him in half over the ATV. His arms flail wildly as the alligator thrashes. Above the horrible screams—Judge's, Charity's, her own—Max hears Eli yell, "Go! Go! Go!"

She races with them all toward the door, looking back only for a second to catch a glimpse of Judge. His body has gone limp, and his arms aren't moving. Eli shoves Max outside. Charity lingers too at the threshold, with Sabine's face planted in her shoulder, and Max grabs her hand to tug them outside.

"Time to be gone!" Eli shouts, and he leads them to the Odenkirks' short white bus. As they all clamber inside, Max notices that the water has already reached the second step. The bus is basically a boat with wheels.

"Oh, sweet Lord," Charity says. "Judgment." She drops onto her knees in the aisle and Sabine scrambles away from her, running to join her assorted cousins. Max stands behind her, looking at the dirty and scared faces of the children. When she locates Sabine, she lifts the backpack from her thin shoulders, feels the familiar weight of what's inside. "You did good," she says.

"So did you," Sabine tells her.

Something unfamiliar swells in Max's heart. She wants to linger in the feeling, but she's knows there is more to be done. At the front of the bus, Eli has lowered Sweeney into one of the seats. Charity slides behind the big steering wheel and leans into it for a second as if she's about to pass out.

"Where's Uncle J.J.?" one of the kids asks.

Charity lifts her face and raises an open hand. "Stop. No questions now. We've got to drive."

Sweeney coughs and says, "That's an awfully damn good idea, I think. I'm in need of the first-aid kit at my place. Be okay once we get there." His face is pale, and he looks at Eli and Max. "I'll be good here, direct this bunch. With the water, I figure ETA about twenty minutes. You two follow in my truck, okay?"

"You bet," Eli says.

Max settles one hand on Charity's shoulder. She feels her trembling. "Are you all right?"

Charity nods. "Guess I'm gonna have to be for a little while longer."

Max is surprised when Charity shifts in the driver's seat and rises to hug her. They embrace, shoulders on chins, and Charity whispers, "Thank you for taking care of Sabine. She's special to me."

Max feels a strange kinship with Charity, a sisterhood of sorts, and tells her, "That girl's special, period."

Charity says, "Ya'll should get in the truck. I know where he lives."

"Right," Eli says. He nods to Sweeney. "See you at your place."

Weakly, Sweeney smiles back. His eyes slowly close, but Max sees he's still breathing fine.

Charity swings open the door and Eli rushes into the storm. Max turns to her a final time and says, "I'm sorry about your brother."

"He made his own choices. I'm got more tears for my momma. She don't deserve this."

Max swallows. The image of Mother Evangeline being swallowed by high waves troubles her. The woman is demented, for sure, and dangerous, but Max sees her for a second only as a mother who loves her children. A mother who above all tried to keep her family together, one who stayed. And the thing is decided. "Yeah. I might go see about that."

Charity studies her. "Don't you do nothing crazy."

"I think that train left town," Max says. "We'll see you at Sweeney's."

Outside the bus, Max has to tug her legs through the high waves, which seem determined to drag her back into the store. At Sweeney's truck, she opens the driver's side door and sees Eli behind the steering wheel. "Move your scrawny ass over," she tells him. "I'm driving."

"Says who?" Eli asks, though he slides to his right. He jostles something and then lifts the ugliest cat Max has ever seen up onto his lap.

Max answers, "Says you're half-blind and have been beat about dead from the looks of it. I could say the same thing for that mangy cat. You sure it's even alive?"

"Mostly," Eli says.

Max shimmies in behind the wheel. She's got the backpack on her lap now, with her arms through the straps in addition to the life vest. Eli says, "That don't look real comfortable. Give it here."

Max holds up a hand. "I'll keep it. You get back in the bus. Go on."

"Back in the bus why?"

"I can handle this truck. I'll be fine," she tells him, not looking his way.

Eli squints his one good eye. "What's this about?"

Max sets her hands on the steering wheel, still staring out into the rain. "I'm headed down to the Chains. Big Momma, she's still alive."

"Mother Evangeline?"

"Crazy as she is, I can't leave her out there like that. Not when there's a chance. You and that Sweeney guy, you came back for me."

Eli shakes his head. "You're one to talk about crazy. This is nuts."

Max says, "I've made enough wrong choices, Eli. I was a royal bitch to Angie and a selfish brat to my dad. No better than my mother. Since I been on this island, I've seen a better way. Think about the chance Charity took, letting us go, giving us that girl. And I watched you climb out on the bridge. I knew what that meant. Even Sweeney, who was safe from this storm — look what he risked to try to save a total stranger. I'm ready to get something right. Know what I mean?"

Eli nods, slow and deep. He lifts his eyes and says, "Damn straight I do. I'm with you."

The bus pulls alongside them. The horn honks twice. Eli sighs and says, "Hang on now." He grabs the cat and climbs out, leaving the door open. Moments later, he comes back empty-handed and says, "Gave her to the kid. Said it was a friend for Jasper." Max gives him a look, and Eli explains, "No point three of us getting killed."

As the bus rumbles into the island's interior, Max watches its taillights grow dimmer. Then she swings the truck around and heads for Infinity Road, aimed at the Chains. Next to her, Eli shakes his head and grins. "I'm not entirely sure I didn't like you better when you were selfish."

Chapter Thirteen

MAYBE THE SHACKS JUST MAKES PEOPLE CRAZY. CHEMICALS in the air, some ancient voodoo curse. But when I think about the kinds of folks who live out here—the Odenkirks, Sweeney, me—there's hardly a sane one in the bunch. So maybe back when she lived in New Jersey, Max was something like normal. Or at least as normal as a girl with green hair can be. Whatever the case may be, this thing she's doing now, driving into rising floodwaters on some half-assed rescue attempt, that's certifiably insane. So make no doubt about it. She's one of us now.

I'm not claiming I don't get what drives her. What she said before, about doing the right thing, making the better choice, that struck some chord in me. Like Max, I'm no fan of my life as it is. But it's not like you can just trade in the one you got for a different one. You're bound tight to your mistakes and your sins, and these are the things that make you who you are.

Take this little field trip to the Chains. Could turn out to be a mistake that makes me dead.

As we drive west, neither one of us says much about the hundred-mile-an-hour winds howling like a pack of banshees, or the rain so thick the windshield wipers are useless. We don't mention the waves banging into either side of the Humvee, rocking the truck like a kid's bath toy, or the water that's sloshing under our feet. And we don't talk about all that happened back at the Sportsman's Castle, or what's waiting for us ahead. We each guzzle a bottle of water from the backpack. I force down a silvery pouch of Chicken Burrito Bombshell, shocked at the awful taste of the soupy stuff, and Max passes when I offer her a Swedish Meatball Madness. Other than this, we just plow west.

Max leans over the dashboard, strangling the steering wheel. Her eyes go from squinting to wide, and she slams the brakes, snapping me forward into the dashboard. I look up through the sheets of rain into the dim shine of our half-submerged headlights. A dozen oil drums ride up and down, bobbing in the waves. One bounces into the front grille and quarter panel, harmless, and then the storm splits them even, driving some inland and sucking the others out to sea. That's how random these waters are ebbing and flowing now, pulling every which way.

After the road is clear, Max accelerates slow, and I lift my feet from the water, which smells of salt and brine. "We're gonna need a bilge pump if this gets much worse."

"Pretty good bet it's not going to get better," Max says. "And I don't know what a bilge pump is."

I tell her it doesn't matter, then I ask a question that's been lingering. "Back at the Castle, how exactly did Charity's ATV end up on the wrong side of the door?"

Max shrugs. "We needed to be inside, and I didn't have a key handy."

"You just smashed into it?"

"I'd like to think of it as a controlled collision."

"Think of it however you want to. It's damn crazy, if you ask me."

"I didn't ask you. At that particular point, I'd come to the conclusion you were pretty much dead."

There's something in her voice — the usual sarcasm, yes, but also some hurt. I say, "Figure I came about as close as I want to."

She opens her mouth to speak, but then catches herself. We drive on, guessing where the road is only by where the houses are along the side, or the occasional parked car. Now and then I say "a little left" or "come on to the right." At one point, a small white shape drifting toward us looks like something I know it can't be. "That an iceberg?" I ask.

Max squints and shakes her head. "Honda."

For a second, I'm fool enough to hope those knucklehead brothers got their momma unstuck, that we can all turn east and head to Sweeney's. But the Honda is empty, and it bobs aimlessly into our lane.

"Back up," I tell her, even as she's shifting gears. In reverse, we rumble about twenty feet, enough to let the abandoned car pass.

"Unbelievable," Max says, and together we watch the storm draw it out into the water. Most likely it'll sink, but I imagine it washed up on a far-off Mexican beach. Waves rock into the driver's side of the Humvee and then, not long after, another bangs into my door. Celeste is punching two-fisted now. Not long after we start moving again, Max says, "So listen. About before, back on the bridge."

She falls quiet, and I know she means for me to speak. "I was there," I say. "What about it?"

"What happened?" she snaps.

"The wind caught ahold of me," I tell her. "Blew my ass into the water, and I nearly drowned." Images of what came next — my visit to the lighthouse, the way I ended up on the other side of the intercostal, the control booth — flicker through my mind, but she doesn't need to know any of that. "I didn't think that was a mystery."

Her face is all scrunched up. "That's not what I mean. Before that. When you were just holding on to the side, you started yelling the hurricane's name."

"I wasn't calling the hurricane. I was calling my big sister."

"Huh," Max says. "That'd be the dead one, right?"

"Only one I got."

She seems unfazed by this. "So what kind of sister was this Celeste?" she asks.

"She was the best," I tell her. "As good a sister as you could ask for. Always took me with her on hikes around the island, taught me how to spot birds, helped me with algebra, looked out for me around town. Used to read to me from her history and travel books. When I was real little, Celeste was the first person I wanted to see my new Lego creations, and later, the first one I showed my drawings."

"You didn't tell me you were an artist," Max says.

"I didn't claim to be an artist," I say back. "I just draw."

"Don't be so damn touchy. Celeste sounds pretty cool."

"More than cool. She was absolutely awesome."

"So you were, like, calling for her help or something?"

"Nothing like that." I shift in my seat, rearrange my legs. But the decision to go on isn't a choice I wrestle with. The words just come. "It's like the Odenkirks were saying, Max. Sometimes she comes to me."

Max taps the brakes and stops the truck. She turns to me. "So you're telling me you really see your sister's ghost?"

"She tends to show up when things are going good, like I'm about to be happy or achieve something. The bridge is a good example. Celeste likes to remind me how I mostly screw things up."

"That doesn't sound so absolutely awesome," Max says.

I throw her a look. "Well, it's complicated."

I'm thinking now of the charcoal-sketch nature of my sister's spirit and how, when I got knocked on my skull, my dreamy vision was the same kind of thing.

"Complicated's a funny word," Max says. "I'm not sure I understand."

"A shrink up in Lake Charles told me it was all in my head, a manifestation of associative guilt or some crap like that. But I don't know. Fact of the matter is, over the years, Celeste has been visiting me, I've kind of gotten used to her. It started right after she died."

"The lighthouse accident," Max says, nodding like she's fitting together puzzle pieces.

"Yeah," I say. "The accident."

"What?" Max asks. "Why'd you say it that way?"

"Let's just drive," I tell her. "Haven't you got more important things to do than interrogate me?"

Her eyes tighten, and I see I hurt her feelings. After she starts us forward again, she says, "No need to get all pissy with me, Eli. Whatever land mine I just stepped on, I'm not the one who planted it."

I cross my arms and push back into the seat.

"Fine by me," she says, and we move forward into the flood.

Now my head's all a mess, and I can't pull free of the lighthouse, what happened on the rocks below. The memory of it all is swarming around me like the hurricane, crowding in. I press my palms on either side of my head, like I'm trying to crush those thoughts, and Max says quietly, "Whatever it is, you can tell me."

Instead of answering her, though, I ask a question of my own. "That time you screwed up your dad's wedding. Would you figure that's the very worst thing you ever did?"

She considers this, and a smirk forms on her lips. "Hard to say," she tells me. "The list of contenders is pretty long when I think about it."

This makes me smile. "Before, when you were talking

about all the bad choices you made. How do you get over them?"

A wave washes into us, and water gushes at our feet, ankle-deep. If it gets much higher, the engine will get swamped and we'll be stranded. Still, she drives. It's like we're committed to this, fated to go forward. Max says, "I'm not sure it's a question of getting *over* anything. Maybe it's just a matter of getting on with it, moving to the next thing."

"What? You just forget?"

"No," she says. One hand reaches for the backpack on her stomach, and she holds tight to what's inside. "You never forget. That's not the way I'd put it."

"Well, how would you say it?"

She squints hard, like she's searching for her next words out in the storm. And then her eyes snap open and she says, "Holy crap."

When I look where she's looking, I'm not sure what it is I see. At this end of the Chains, on the ramp that leads down from the main road to the crossway, a set of headlights aims up into the midnight-black sky. The grille of the Odenkirks' Ford pickup rises out of the water, but the bed is totally submerged. It looks like a dog struggling to keep from drowning. Behind it in the surf is Mother Evangeline's silver egg trailer, turned sideways and free-floating on the rolling surface. The hole cut in the side, the one I walked through earlier in the day, is facing up. How it's not sunk, I got no idea. As we drive closer, I can see Percy Odenkirk standing in the truck's bed, even there up to his knees in the water. The trailer swings wildly to the right, then snaps to the left, yanked by the waves.

"Get as close as you can," I tell Max. "But don't drive down."

"Good advice," she says.

We park almost bumper to bumper with the Ford, and get out into four feet of water. "Keep hold on something, or you'll get washed away for sure," I yell into the thunderous howling.

At the front of Sweeney's Humvee, I reach just under the water and take hold of the tow hook at the end of the winch line. I heave it along with me, unwinding wire as I walk along the Ford, Max on the opposite side. When we near Percy in the truck bed, he grabs his thick hair and hollers, "Momma and Obie! Out in that thing!"

"All right," I say. "Hold tight."

"The truck's dead! Help us!" he screams, jumping down and taking hold of my shirt. It seems clear Percy's come undone a bit. I tell him to go sit in the Humvee and wait for me to give him the signal, which gets him out of our way.

From the other side of the bed, Max says, "Why don't we just tow them both out?"

"Too heavy for the winch," I tell her. "Especially in all this water. Watch that chain! It's got half a mind to rip your legs off."

The chain in question—between the Ford and the trailer—is like a ten-foot leash, the trailer like a yard dog trying to break free. The links attached to the floating trailer are above water, but they dip below the surface along the way back to the truck, where the chain must be hooked to the submerged hitch. As the trailer sways, it rips the chain back and forth.

"So what's the plan?" she yells.

"That chain's tugged way too tight to undo right now. I'm gonna try to hook this into the trailer chain." I hold up the little grappling hook for show and tell. "Then we let the Humvee's winch take the weight. Once we got us a little slack, we unhook the chain from the pickup, winch the trailer off that ramp, try to hook her up to the Humvee. After that, haul ass."

"Good plan," she shouts. "I hope we're not hauling corpses."

From fifteen feet away, there's a shrill cry in the storm, and we turn to see Obie sticking his bald head out from the top of the sideways trailer. He's waving his arms like a drowning man, though that trailer's floating pretty good. Lord knows how.

"What's he saying?" Max asks.

"Can't hear him," I tell her. "But it's a good bet it's a variation on 'get us the hell out of here.'"

"Let's get to it."

I can't attach the hook too low on the chain or else the truck's position won't let us pull forward enough. But the chain is like a string holding a kite in a crazy wind—totally unpredictable. With one hand steady on the tailgate of the pickup, the other clutches the grappling hook, just waiting for a shot. That chance comes just after a large wave swoops in, raising up to our necks, then rushes inland. In its wake, there's a little lull, and the trailer drifts toward us, a lucky break. This makes the whole chain go loose, and in an instant, I change plans. We can do this all at once.

Splashing forward, I holler, "Unhook it! At the truck, the truck!" and I reach underwater for the slack chain. I grasp it, tugging a section up to the surface, and Max is scrambling back at the trailer hitch, shoving her arms under but keeping her head above the water. "Can't find it!" I hear her yell. Carefully, I ease one curling hook through a single link in the chain, like threading a great metal needle, and drop it. "I'm on," I say, wading fast back to her, swinging my arms and kicking my legs. The water's still sort of calm, and I don't understand or care why. The trailer's bobbing along toward us, so near now I can actually hear Obie, though I can't make out his words. Max says, "Here! Here!" and I'm at her side, my hands sliding along her arm down underwater, and my fingers feel for the S-shaped hook at the end of the chain that gets slipped through the tow hole. But all I feel is links of chain and the bumper. Where they meet, there's a hard lumpy mess, rocky, like something melted.

Now the sounds Obie's making come clear. I straighten, dread dropping in my gut, and tell Max what he's saying, why he's waving his arms like that. "It's welded on," I say. "The damn tow chain's welded to the truck!"

"How do we get it off?" she shouts.

I shake my head. "We can't. Not at this end."

I can see it dawn in her eyes, the reality of what I'm telling her. And just as this sinks in, as my mind's telling my legs to rush back and unhook the grappler, I figure out why the water's gone calm. A low-pitched growl from the gulf side cuts under the wind's wicked howling. I know its source before I turn, but even so I'm not ready for what I see.

A thirty-foot tall wave rumbles our way. It's a rushing wall of tumbling water, capped by white foam. Like the devil come for his due, the storm surge has arrived.

I grab hold of Max, wrapping one wrist around a backpack strap. She says, "What are you—" and we're blindsided by the wall of water. It sweeps us both sideways, rolling us upside down and trying to tug us apart. There's no air, no earth, and I kick my legs to fight a current determined to suck me down with a riptide's strength. I feel my lungs burn, and that backpack strap bites into my wrist, but I hold fast. Suddenly, my head breaks the surface, and I'm gulping for oxygen. Next to me, Max floats faceup. I take hold of her life vest and shake. "Hey! Hey! You with me?"

"I'm here," she says, looking more surprised than anything. "Where's the Humvee?"

I try to lift my head and take in what's around us, but the waves are five-footers easy. "All I see is water."

"Where's the land?" she yells.

"Under us now, I think. We need to swim." I swivel my head, looking for something to help me get my bearings. But there's nothing. In all this drowning darkness, I can't even guess my directions. Besides, exhausted as I am, I doubt I could doggy-paddle the length of a pool. Only clutching Max's life vest is keeping me from going under.

Just then we hear a cry in the wind. "Mercy, Lord! Mercy on your servant!"

We both turn to locate Mother Evangeline, who is somehow bobbing along on the swells, not but twenty feet away.

"Come on!" Max shouts, and together we start fighting our way to her. As we near her, she keeps praying, and what I see makes less and less sense. Her entire upper body is out of the water, and her huge fleshy arms are draped over something long and rectangular. Only when we reach her do I realize what's keeping her afloat: her husband's coffin.

We both take hold too, me and Max across from Mother Evangeline, all of us now clinging to the wooden box. Looking at Max with a strangely satisfied grin, she shouts, "So it is as I foresaw. I knew we would face the storm together."

In a loud voice, Max asks, "Any chance you saw us getting rescued?"

"Where are my boys?" she yells back. "Obie and Percy, they were trying to save me."

Neither one of us can think of anything to say. There's no way to tell where they are, but my guess is they didn't make it. I'm afraid we'll be joining them soon enough. Judging by Max's face, she's thinking the same thoughts as I am. My feet stretch out for solid ground and find nothing, and the swirling current is dragging us hard. I turn to Max. "Just hold on," I tell her. "Don't let go. That storm surge is the worst of it for now, and we survived."

What I don't tell her about is the cruddy feeling in my

gut. I got no hard evidence, no compass to prove what I'm thinking. But I'm pretty sure Celeste is sucking us out to sea.

It's not long before Mother Evangeline starts in singing hymns. A couple I recognize from mass at St. Jude's like "Breathe on Me, Oh Breath of God," and "There's a Wideness in God's Mercy." Others I never heard before. But they're all pretty much the same, songs about the greatness of the Almighty Lord, the messed-up nature of man, and the saving grace of Christ. As we get pelted by the rain and tossed by the waves, she belts them out loud and off-key, maybe hoping God or Jesus or her dead husband hears her over the wind, which is screaming like a freight train. At one point in the concert, Max asks her if she does requests, but Mother Evangeline ignores her and launches into "What a Friend We Have in Jesus." In between songs, she speaks to Aloysius, asking him if he remembers when they first met, if he regretted following the crooked path. This whole while, we're swirling around on a rollicking ocean beneath a gray sky, and there's no sign of land.

The hulking shadow appears like a dream, or maybe a mirage would be a better way to put it. But in the rolling black world, quite suddenly I'm aware of a darker shape rising from the waves, and it looks stable, solid. "You see that?" I shout to Max, who's got her head planted between crossed arms. She lifts it and looks, and Mother Evangeline stops mid-lyric. I say, "Could be an oil platform."

"Whatever it is," Max says, "I vote we make a break for it."

"No, child!" Mother Evangeline insists. "It's a temptation. The four of us should stay together."

"We're only three," I nearly say, then I realize how unhelpful that would be, so I keep my math to myself.

"Aloysius is certain salvation will come our way. God will send us a sign."

The waves—each one maybe ten feet tall—roller-coaster us up and down, but gradually push us closer to whatever it is. After a few swells, I place the familiar outline. "It's the *Capricornia*," I yell. "The casino boat that got scuttled off the coast. That's as good a sign as God's likely to send."

"Don't mock the Lord," Mother Evangeline says from the coffin's other side.

I try to explain to her. "The hurricane's dragging us into the gulf. We're all getting weaker by the minute. If we don't get off this thing, we'll die. Now kick toward it!"

Mother Evangeline shakes her jowly face. "We can't abandon Aloysius. Even the dead don't never die. They just take on new form."

Max says, "Me, I like the form I got just fine." Together me and her lean into the wooden casket and start thrashing our legs, twin Evinrudes on the back of a johnboat. But who knows if we're making any difference? The coffin rotates all on its own, it seems, ebbing and flowing with every wave whichever way it feels like. On top of that, I hear Mother Evangeline grunting and realize she's swinging her own hefty legs, probably the first exercise she's done in a decade. The only thing is, she's pushing into us from her side of the coffin, trying to drive us away from the boat.

"Are you serious?" I shout at her.

"You can't resist God's plan. Aloysius is certain we should stay together. We must!"

"Stay if you need to," Max yells. "I'm heading for that boat."

"Don't go, child!" Mother Evangeline begs.

"We can't leave her," I holler to Max.

She turns to me, holds my eyes with hers, and says, "At this point, we aren't leaving her, Eli. She's staying. There's a difference. She's made her choice. You need to make yours." With that, she lifts her hands from the coffin, and instantly the storm sweeps her away. Even with the orange life vest, she looks to be drowning, arms flailing in the whitewater. That boat seems far off.

Evangeline lurches forward, clasping a hand over my forearm. "Stay," she begs. "God's reward is here with me!"

I hesitate, looking at the deep need in her face, then place my free hand atop hers, which is cold and clammy. She takes this as an act of reassurance and smiles. Only when I start to pry her fingers away from my wrist does that smile tighten. She pleads for me to stop, praying for Jesus to give me strength. Some dark part of me, the part that felt empty, does want to float away with this crazy old bat and drown like a martyr. But deeper down, something else — some finer impulse — has begun to glow. The waters suck my legs away from the coffin, but my grip on Mother Evangeline keeps me anchored. She knows what I'm going to do and shakes her head. "No! You mustn't! You can't!"

"I'm sorry," I say. "I want to live." And when I release, the waves pull me free, out into the ocean.

Tossed and swamped by the rollicking water, I spot a bit of orange ahead of me and try to aim myself its way. But swimming in these waters feels a bit like jogging through an earthquake. Some larger force like gravity's got ahold of me—yanking me with an invisible hand—and I'm not convinced my kicking and splashing's doing anything more than wearing me out. I lose sight of the boat, then catch it again in a fleeting glimpse as I crest another wave. Then one crashes over me, and I'm swallowed by the ocean. I burst to the surface choking up salt water. I feel heavy and tired, but I keep swimming hard as I'm able, for longer than I thought possible.

Little by little, the boat gets bigger, and then I hear Max's voice hollering, "Come on! Here! Come on!" It's there before me now, looming like a cliff, and Max splashes into the water at my side. She grabs me and heaves me forward. A wave slams us into something hard, and we're scrambling together up under a railing, rolling onto a deck of some sort. There's water still, water sloshing all around us, but we're out of the waves.

After all that tumbling and tossing, it feels weird to have something solid beneath my feet again, and I feel dizzy as I rise up on wobbly knees, holding tight to the rail. Max stands at my side, and I half fall into her, wrapping my arms around her vest. To keep me from falling, she hugs me back, and together we squint through the rain, out into the dark ocean. In the distance, somehow I see Mother Evangeline still riding that coffin, still clinging hard to all that was, even as it draws her to her doom. And I hear her voice, offering up a song of praise or petition or both. I can't make out the words.

Chapter Fourteen

WITHOUT A LIFE JACKET, ELI HAD A ROUGHER TIME THAN Max did with the swim from coffin to casino boat. Next to her at the rail, his body slumps forward, as if he might collapse. So she makes herself a human crutch, draping one of his arms around her neck and having him lean into her for support. After Mother Evangeline has vanished from view, Max guides them along the slick deck, gripping the wet railing. The gulf sloshes up over the sides, spilling cold water across their feet, and she's surprised the ocean isn't higher. They come across a set of double doors with a dollar sign across the split, emblazoned with the words FEEL LIKE A WINNER? When she rears back and drives her foot into them, they burst inward, and Max feels lucky indeed.

Inside, the storm is still loud, but the deafening crash is muted enough that there's some relief. From her backpack, she pulls out a glow stick, rips the black foil, shakes it good. It comes to life and casts a pale green aura on their immediate surroundings. They pass a cashier's cage and walk along a row of slot machines. Max can tell that in full light, the colors would all be gaudy, a rainbow of tacky brightness. She stumbles and thinks it must be because of her exhaustion, plus the weight of a boneless Eli. But then she notices that the cheap chandeliers hang slanted from the ceiling, which means the floor beneath her might well be tilted. She navigates through a blackjack pit and finally deposits Eli on a roulette table, dumping his limp body across the felt as if he were a drunk. His head thwacks the table hard, and Max quickly unbuckles her life vest, lifts his head gently, and sets the spongy material underneath. Eli smiles and says, "Much obliged."

She studies his battered face, that one eye nothing but a bruise. "You've been beat down hard today, got tossed off a bridge, and nearly drowned twice that I know of. Now we're on a shipwrecked casino boat in the heart of a hurricane. I figured you could use a hand."

With what looks like considerable effort, he lifts an arm and sets his hand along her neck. "Hey, Jersey Girl. You just said 'figured.'"

From beneath them a deep groan sounds, like wood straining under too much weight. "What's that?" she asks.

"Probably a killer whale come to eat us, way things been going," Eli says, and Max's eyes widen. He says, "Just messing. That's this old boat registering her complaint about all the abuse."

"But it came from under us."

"This isn't the first floor," he tells her. "She's half-underwater. We're not floating on account of that big hole in her bow from when she scuttled. Go down those steps and you'll find yourself in an aquarium."

Max thinks about all that water, rushing through the boat beneath them, and the wind outside beating at its walls. Another sound, this one like a huge hinge creaking, splits the air around them. "How much more can a boat like this take?"

"I guess we'll find that out. But we're better off now than we were on that coffin."

"I guess so."

"No need to guess. I'm telling you." He lets go of her neck and reaches back to touch the life vest he's using as a pillow. "Likely as not we'll be going in the water again, and it'd be good to have a couple of them on hand. You think you could go look around for some on the deck?"

Max nods. "For sure. You all right on your own?"

"I'm fine. Or I will be soon enough. Just drank me a little too much ocean."

Max isn't sure about leaving Eli, not just because she's worried about him but because she has mixed feelings about being alone. She looks at his face, where now both eyes have eased shut and his mouth is open in slow breathing. Shrugging her arms free of the straps, she deposits the backpack on the table next to his legs, then shakes out a second glow stick to leave with him.

Max crosses the casino floor, which even now feels a little more crooked than it did just minutes ago. If she dropped an eight ball, it might roll back in the direction she came. Rain sprays through the doors she kicked open, and before she strides out into the storm, she tucks her face into her shoulder and takes a deep breath, as if she's about to leap from the high dive. Maybe the ocean has claimed a bit more of the ship and maybe she's just imagining it, but either way, the water covering the deck isn't enough to really slow her down. She's careful and holds tight to the railing, pulling herself along arm over arm. The storm drives wind into her face, slaps her cheeks with rain. She hunches and keeps moving.

By a porthole, the shine of the glow stick illuminates a fire extinguisher next to a bolted notice with the warning signs of gambling addiction. Not long after, dark shapes curl along the white wall, what at first she takes for vines. But upon closer inspection, she makes out loopy cursive letters spray-painted by some adventurous soul. "Heather and Blake Forever!" the graffiti reads.

As Max presses on, her mind strangely fixates on this couple, teenagers for sure, who used the boat not as a refuge from a storm but a romantic hideaway. Together maybe they rowed one of those skinny pirogues out here, away from the petty troubles of their daily lives.

Max reaches a rectangular pool of water, which she realizes can only be a flooded staircase. The handrail she's holding angles down into the rollicking water. There's a wall beyond this point, so she can go no farther, and it's only when she turns that she sees a life preserver hanging over a white box, next to a sign that points into the flooded stairwell and reads THIS WAY TO MORE LUCKY WINNING!

Max leans over the white box and reaches for the life preserver, the old-fashioned circular kind, but she finds it stuck fast to the wall. Even tugging with her hands on either side fails to free it, and she probes the rim for some sort of safety latch or trigger. When she doesn't find one, she hurries back to the fire extinguisher and returns. Hoisting it to shoulder height, Max pounds its rounded edge down onto the preserver. On the fifth blow, it breaks off, taking part of the plaster with it. This makes no sense until Max sees the pointy screws emerging from the preserver's back. It's a replica, a fake symbol of a nostalgic nautical past.

Exhausted and angry, Max slumps on the white box, holding the useless life preserver. Only then does she see the small red letters stenciled neatly on the top of the box, OPEN ONLY IN CASE OF EMERGENCY. She flings the fake preserver into the riotous ocean and lifts the plywood cover. Inside she finds not just one orange life vest but a whole stack of them, and off to the side, something else, an unexpected treasure. She grabs the canvas handle, and though she's surprised by its heft, she can't help but glance up at the THIS WAY TO MORE LUCKY WINNING! sign, which turned out to be prophetic.

When she gets back to Eli, she finds him not at the roulette table where she left him but twenty feet away, standing before a huge spinning wheel. In one hand, he holds his glow stick like a lantern. Leaving the bag under the roulette table, she goes to him, arriving just as he's spinning again. "Any luck?" he asks.

She nods. "And then some. What's this?"

Eli shrugs. "Just checking to see if I'm a billionaire."

The wheel slows, and Max can read what's written inside each pie-shaped section as it buzzes past. Most of the big ones are two or five dollars, but there's a thin slice with fifty dollars and even one with a hundred dollars. "The house always wins," she says. "All these things are rigged."

"Those are the odds," he agrees. "But sometimes you get lucky."

Together they watch the wheel slow. The red pointer clacks along the metal pins circling the rim, gradually coming to a full stop in one of the many slots marked TRY AGAIN!

"Not this time," Max says.

Eli waves his hand at it. "Just a game. You and me, we got other odds to think on."

Max says, "Well, they got a little better just now. Come on."

She leads him back to the roulette table and shows off the life jackets she's retrieved. "All right," Eli says, sliding his arms through one and fastening the straps.

Max gets back into the one she swiped from Sportsman's Castle. "Now we're officially all ready not to drown." Eli chuckles a bit, and Max pulls out the canvas bag, the size of a small suitcase.

"What you got there?" Eli asks, eyebrows spiked in curiosity.

"It's a major prize," she tells him. "Everyone's a winner."

Using both hands, she hoists the bag up onto the roulette table, then borrows Eli's glow stick and holds it with hers, creating a ball of yellow-green light. "Here now," she says, illuminating the label she saw earlier. She reads EMERGENCY INFLATABLE FLOTATION UNIT.

Eli looks at her with his one good eye. "I'll be damned," he says. "My dad told me about these things. They've got them out on the oil platforms, federal regulations, crazy expensive. They're near impossible to sink."

"But it's just a raft, right? Once we're back out in that storm, who knows where it'll go?"

"Not being able to steer is a considerable disadvantage. But I can't quite believe this casino boat's got much life left to give."

Above them, a great ripping sound draws their eyes up. All the chandeliers shiver a bit, like there'd just been a tremor. Max imagines the roof peeling back, but the ceiling stays where it is. She says, "Just how long is a hurricane like this supposed to last?"

Eli scratches the back of his neck. "We got no way of knowing what's happened with the storm. Figure she made landfall just after the storm surge. If she's skirting the coast and we're in an outer edge—which would be really lucky—she might start dying down soon. But if she's passing straight overhead, we could be looking at hours of this."

Along the far wall, a few of the slot machines topple over, crashing to the ground. Max says, "This boat's not going to be here for hours."

"I'm with you on that, though I don't want to take our

chances out there any longer than we need to. That's asking for it." Eli leans in close, so his face is side by side with Max's in the brightness from the glow stick.

They read the short list of instructions printed on the outside of the bag. When she finishes, Max says, "So we split our bets. You stay put. I'm going to tie this thing off and inflate it. It'll be ready for a quick escape if we need it. Like a getaway car."

Eli shrugs. "Best plan we got."

"That seems to be our motto."

"Better I come with you, though. I doubt you got any knots in Jersey like the one you'll need."

She knows it's not worth protesting, so each of them grabs a strap, and together they tug the heavy bag back into the storm. Outside, they each kneel down, tucking their faces against the onslaught of rain, and hook an elbow around the railing as an anchor. Waves crest over the deck now, splashing water across their feet. Max unzips the bag and, hand over hand, tugs out a rope that becomes a tail of sorts. Eli loops it around an intersection of the rails, forming an X, then curls it into itself several times, finally forming an intricate bow.

Max unzips the rest of the bag, then peels down its sides like she's unwrapping a Christmas present. She exposes a bright orange bundle of plastic fabric and locates a rip cord with a wrist strap. She eases her hand through it, rolls her wrist a few times to increase her purchase, then motions to Eli for them to lift the bundle together. They heave it up on the top of the railing and dump it over the side, though it has only a few feet to fall till it plops into the ocean. A wave nearly washes it back over the railing, but then it drifts away, drawing out both the leash tied to the railing and the rip cord. When it goes tight, Max wastes no time, snapping her end hard.

Almost instantly, the bundle begins to unfurl. It reminds her of some kind of stop-motion animation, the jerky rapid motion, like a flower bulb blooming in mere moments. One edge flops open, then the other, and the boat takes shape as a twelve-foot octagon. Like their life vests, it is bright orange and puffy. The lifeboat bobs along the surface, snapping and tugging against the rope like a living thing straining to escape. It's secure for now.

Back inside the casino, Max retrieves the backpack, and the two of them settle into a corner just inside the door, wanting to be close in case they need to make a break for it. They sit on the floor side by side.

For a while, they say nothing, and Max thinks of asking Eli about his sister again, or getting back to the worst thing she ever did. She can see his tilted head dipping toward his chest, and even his one good eye is half-closed. Still, she can't help but ask the question that's loudest in her mind. "Eli, you think we'll die out here?"

He rights his head, swallows, and blinks. "We might not. Crazier things have happened." He forces a smile.

"Coming here," Max says out of the blue. She lifts the backpack, heavy with her father's urn. "Stealing this."

"What now?" Eli asks.

"Back in the truck. You wanted to know the worst thing I ever did. That was it. My dad loved Angie and she loved him back. Now she's got no way to do what she needs to do. I was stupid and selfish." She doesn't say, *Just like my mom*, but the words drive into her mind like spikes. For years, she's viewed her father's second marriage as an echo of her mother's betrayal, that her dad was unfaithful to the family. Now it suddenly seems clear to Max that in fact, she's the one who was untrue. Like her mom, Max took off when she was needed. The tears come quick and hard, and before Max can stop it, she's sobbing.

She buries her face in both hands, trembling and shaking. When she feels Eli's arm settle over her shoulder and his gentle squeeze, she shrugs and brushes it off. But he persists, and they huddle into each other on the floor. "All you can do is try to make it right," he says. "Try to fix whatever is broke."

Max imagines Angie, a pregnant widow dressed in black, her shattered face hidden behind a veil.

"No point beating yourself up like this," Eli tells her. "Everybody screws up."

Max shakes her head. "Not like I did."

A chandelier crashes to the floor, rattling them both, and they clutch tighter. When they ease up, Eli says, "No, not like you did. Some folks do even worse."

Max lifts her face to look at his. "Come again?"

"My sister," he says. "She didn't fall." His expression is flat, numb. "What happened up the lighthouse wasn't no accident. She wanted to be done, and I watched her do it. I didn't try to stop her."

"She jumped?" Max asks, instantly regretting the dumb question.

Eli nods his head slightly, staring across the tilted casino floor. "That's why she's sticking around all this time. 'Cause she's mad."

"Mad for what?"

"Mad that I didn't do more."

Now Max straightens, kneeling up next to the sitting Eli. "What more do you expect she wanted you to do? Weren't you just a boy?"

He meets her eyes with his. "I was her brother," he says. "That means I was supposed to protect her."

Max realizes she's stopped crying at the same time she sees that Eli's cheeks are beginning to glisten. She says, "You can't protect somebody from themselves. Look at Mother Evangeline. Celeste is the one that made her decision. Not you."

Eli looks away. "I guess."

"No need to guess," Max says, repeating Eli's line. "I'm telling you how it is."

This makes him smile. They are quiet for a bit while Max's mind works something over. "So she saw you there and still jumped? She knew you'd see her do it?"

"Yeah," Eli says.

"That's pretty messed up. She had to know it would get in your head. Your sister, she must've been in a damn dark place."

"She was. More than I understood. I knew the real Celeste, full of love and light."

"Yeah," Max repeats. "Love and light."

"What?" Eli asks.

Max hesitates. "Nothing. It's just—well, if what you say is true and she was all full of sweetness and cuddles, how come her ghost is such a bitch?"

Eli's face goes expressionless. He looks at Max but makes no reply.

"Really," Max presses, "what's with the world's best sister always putting you down like you were saying? How does that even start to make sense?"

"What's your point?" he asks.

"No point. Just putting a question out there."

She can tell this is unsettling Eli, and he withdraws the arm he had draped over her shoulder. He curls away from her, into the corner, and closes his good eye, letting his chin settle down onto his chest. "You're just making my head hurt more. Lay off, all right?"

Max feels bad and considers apologizing, but instead of saying anything else, she slides over alongside him. She presses into his back and stretches one arm across him. He doesn't pull away. She feels his chest rise and fall, and she wonders if he's slipped back asleep. Outside, the wind shrieks and the waves thunder. The *Capricornia*'s floor beneath her quakes, and the chandeliers overhead tremble. Her mind floats elsewhere, to Charity and Sabine, and she tries to picture them inside Sweeney's fortified ranger station. Charity hangs both arms over Sabine, who hugs Jasper to her chest. And that ugly cat curls in a ball next to them all. Then Max imagines Angie back home in Wayne. Has she called off the search for her maniac stepdaughter? Is she packing up her father's clothes to donate to Goodwill, where Max's coworkers will pick through the remnants of his life? And what of his other belongings—will she throw out the pictures of their trip to Louisiana? What will she keep to show the child waiting to be born into the world, fatherless?

A great wave slams the boat's far side as the wind whistles like an incoming bombshell. Another chandelier crashes from the ceiling ten feet away, shattering in a cascade of glass. But Eli doesn't shift. Max looks at his chest—expanding and contracting, laboriously—yet he seems so deep asleep. It gives her some comfort, the idea that he is resting, and she wonders if he might find relief in dreams. She sets one hand gently on his and does not squeeze because just feeling his heat is enough. It's a silly notion, and she recognizes it as such, but Max thinks about Sabine's claim that she could slip into other people's dreams. She closes her eyes and wishes she could fall asleep and somehow join Eli in his troubled dreaming.

Chapter Fifteen

FROM WAY OUT IN THE DARKNESS, SOMEBODY'S HOLLERING my name. A lady or a girl, I can't quite tell. It's not my mom calling me for dinner, or my sister yelling that it's time we finished up our hike and head home. But whoever she is, she's insistent, demanding. As I get to waking, I realize she's rattling my shoulders pretty hard, and Mother Evangeline's face floats past me, then Sabine's. But when I open my eyes, it's Max kneeling over me, her face lit up by the greenish shine of a glow stick. She shouts, "Eli, the boat! The boat!"

I feel foggy and drunk, unable to make sense of all I'm seeing. The mirrored ceiling above bleeds water, streaming down through cracks and fractures. The floor's gone tilted so hard that it's a hill now, and nearly all the slot machines have collapsed. Two more just above us tumble over and slide right by. They rocket past the blackjack tables and splash into a dark pool of gulf water thirty feet below us. I shake my head, barely aware of Max's screaming. She tugs me to my feet, and now I hear her words, "Time to go!"

"Hell yes," I tell her, finally coming around. "Evacuate."

We hold on to each other as we climb the floor, sloped away from the exit. It's a little like the beginning of the end of that goofy *Titanic* movie when the mighty ship splits in two and the floor becomes a wall. Clearly, the *Capricornia*'s lost her final battle with Hurricane Celeste.

The wind is having its way with the double doors, blowing them inward and then sucking them out, like we're inside a huge lung. They strain and rattle against their hinges. "Look out!" Max shouts, holding up an elbow to protect her face as we get near. With her other hand, she's pulling me closer. She reaches for the near door, trying to steady it as it flaps like mad, but I tug her back.

"Don't be a fool!" I yell.

"Little late for that, don't you think?" she says, snapping her wrist free of my grip.

When she goes again to grab the swing door, there's a great ripping sound, like a tree cracking in a thunderstorm, and the door is yanked from the frame, sucked spinning out into the hurricane sky. We move quick through the opening left behind. The rain is thicker than ever, heavy sheets swamping us both. The slicing wind drives us to the railing. If not for it, we'd be flung over the ocean like that door. At first, we both just hold on, lucky we don't go airborne, but then the deck buckles beneath us and the whole boat lurches. I can't be sure, but could be we're starting to spin.

Hand over hand, we drag ourselves up the inclined deck, mountain-climbing along the railing. Only reason I know Max is ahead of me is the weak light of her glow stick, which

I make out when I lift my face into the biting wind. Finally, that glow quits moving in the deluge, and I catch up to her. I look out into the ocean for our escape raft but see only tumbling waves, ten feet tall.

"Here," she shouts, leaning back so I can see what's ahead of her. There's the rope, just exactly as I tied it, secured to the railing. But instead of leading out and down into the water, it leads up onto the roof of the casino boat, taut as a fishing line that's snagged something mean.

We each reach out and take hold of the rope, tug down hard with all our weight to try to flip the raft back down. It doesn't even notice. The wind's beating it back, or maybe it's got hooked on something up there. "Climb up?" I yell.

Max gives me a look, and this time, she's got a point. If either one of us releases our grip on the rope, sure as sin we'd get blown out to sea. Inside my curled fingers, the rope chews the skin. But I don't let go, and neither does Max. Ahead of us, a chunk of the deck just lifts away, weightless, and corkscrews up, vanishing in the rain. We clutch the rope together, side by side, and I'm thinking we've somehow found ourselves ready for last words, if they're to be spoke. "Max!" I holler, and she turns to face me. "I'm real damn sorry." I mean for her to know how much I regret that I was ugly to her when we first met, that I failed to get her to safety by the dumb choices I made.

Who knows if she gets any of that, but she smiles and yells, "Sorry for nothing. We gave this a good fight."

The boat bucks again, like a bronco trying to shake its rider, and the rope rips itself from our grasp. Both of us drop flat to the deck. I roll quick into Max and wrap my arms around her, and we tumble to the side, nearly sliding into the ocean. Right on the edge, Max has grabbed some bit of railing, anchoring us.

When I gaze up, something now hovers in the storm, right above us. Max sees it too, and she yells, "That the raft?"

The big orange inflatable isn't flying away. It's just twirling madly in the wind, like a battered windsock. Celeste's trying to steal the only way out we got left. The crazy image of us climbing the rope straight up flashes in my mind. Instead, we watch it dip down, then strain up, flip around again, all the while tugging to free itself. It's like a tethered bird that's too stupid to know it's not going anywhere. This show goes on for a few minutes, long enough that we finally just tuck our faces into each other and huddle, focused only on not letting go of the railing.

Then the sky collapses.

At least that's what it feels like. The raft flops down on top of us, heavy and wet. It cuts off the rain and quiets the wind some, but it also smothers us. I look over for Max in the dark, worried she's crushed or suffocated. "Ya'll right?" I yell, and she yells back, "Still kicking."

We belly crawl out from under the raft, scrambling for air. I'm surprised we're not even trapped by the weight, which is spongy and soft. Stranger still, though, is that out in the open, the wind's not so strong as it was, and the rain's suddenly about what you'd get during any old thunderstorm. We get to our feet, shaky, and look out over the ocean, where the waves are still fat and high, but the sharp mountain peaks are gone. They look more like rolling hills.

"Just me or is this dying down?" Max asks, putting to words the same question I had.

I shrug and grin. "Guess so. Could be we don't die today."

She spins into me, and we wrap arms around each other. Maybe she starts crying and maybe she doesn't. In just a few minutes, the clouds are breaking overhead, and impossibly, a circle of night sky opens above us. We can see the stars and even the half-moon's bony light. I hear Max curse and turn to see what caught her attention. With the light, I can see the back half of the *Capricornia*, a hundred yards away and on its side. "The storm ripped her in two," I say. "Lucky we didn't roll over."

"Lucky for a lot of reasons," Max answers.

The wind dies down to nothing but a strong breeze, and the rain slows to a drizzle, like somebody's shut off the fan and turned off the spigot.

I take in the damage to the section of the boat we're on. The deck is tilted at about a forty-five-degree angle, with the bow rising above us, the tip of our little island. Overhead, huge chunks of the third floor got ripped loose by Celeste, like something enormous took a few bites of it. Below, where this section of the boat cracked from the other, the wreck rests in the water.

With a moan, the other half of the *Capricornia* crumbles in on itself, going from wrecked riverboat to trash in about five seconds. The waves, small now and almost what I'd call calm, get to dispersing the debris. I say to Max, "No way of knowing how long we got on this thing."

Max looks at the sloped deck beneath us as if trying to gauge its strength. "Search-and-rescue teams?"

I shake my head. "They got a lot on their mind. Celeste's headed to Texas to make trouble now. Behind her, the disaster zone's going to be a hundred square miles. And don't forget, nobody thinks there's anyone down here to save."

As if to add to my argument, a portion of wall below us sags and drops into the water. Pieces of lumber bump into each other.

Max looks at the upside-down raft. "You like our chances in that thing?"

I consider her question and look up at the stars dotting the sky overhead, which is now miraculously cloudless. "I like our odds in that a lot better than here. We grab up some of them boards, paddle toward the land."

Max stares out at the horizon, squinting. "That brings up an obvious question."

I scan the waters in the direction I think is land. Other than the wreckage from the back end of the *Capricornia*, there's nothing save a gray ring of distant clouds. I wonder if we got pushed out to sea, and if so, how far. "C'mon," I say, and we take hold of the railing again to ascend to the crooked bow.

Up at the peak, I see we're not totally hung up. Way off to the right, maybe a few miles, the moonlight shines on the water tower sticking out of the ocean. I strain for the steeple from St. Jude's, which ought to be just a bit closer, but either I can't see it or it isn't there anymore.

"Eli," Max says, touching my shoulder. She points in the other direction. Much closer, maybe only a half mile off, I see the tallest structure of this drowned world. Lucy stands proud and strong, not seeming to notice or care that her base is submerged. I look at the backpack Max is still carrying, think of what's inside and the quest that brought her here. "You up for a quick detour before we head back to civilization?"

She seems to consider this in silence, nibbling on her lip. I add, "You can finish what you started."

Max nods. "I like the sound of that."

Together we make our way down to the life raft, set it right side up, then wrestle it over the railing. It splashes down into the water, then bobs on the surface, trying to float off. With the skin chewed up on my hands, I wince as I hold the rope secure. We give it a few minutes to be sure there's no leak, watching nervously.

Finally, I tell Max, "Okay. All aboard." She slips under the rail, sits on the deck's edge, then shoves herself away from the boat. She lands in the raft like a kid in a moon bounce. The raft, shaped like a stop sign, has got space for a dozen people. The little tent enclosure part has been torn away, but somehow the base is intact. As Max gathers up some drifting boards to use as paddles, I'm thinking what a pain maneuvering her will be, but with the two of us, we'll manage. I figure twenty minutes to the lighthouse, mostly with the tide, then a few hours to town, slow going in the debris without real paddles. Any luck the sun'll be up by then, and we'll survey the damage, search for Sweeney and Charity, then make our way inland to Hackberry. Best bet we come across a shelter or some rescue crew. The day ahead will be long and hard, but with the storm behind us, we're in way better shape now than we've been since we met.

She waves me down and says, "You waiting for an engraved invitation or something? This way the hell out."

"Yeah," I say, and I set my hands on the top rail, still holding the rope, ready to climb over and leap down. Just then, though, a shadow blocks the moonlight and draws my eyes up into the sky. A flock of clouds scoots overhead, and I notice the life raft is getting tossed a bit higher on agitated waves. I look to the horizon, where that dirty wall of swirling gray clouds seems closer now than it was just a few minutes ago. A whole lot closer. Up above, I squint at the patch of open night sky and realize it's a circle.

"Eli!" Max yells. "What's with the face?"

I look at her and see she's still smiling. I tell her, "We're not out of this yet. This is the eye passing over us."

"The eye?"

"A calm zone at the center of the hurricane."

She looks around, holding on to the side to balance as the raft rocks. "You mean it's coming back?"

I shake my head. "I mean it never left. We're in the belly of the beast."

"Well, hell," Max says. "That about sucks. Do we go or stay?"

I look at the remains of the *Capricornia*. "Can't stay. This boat'll never last through act two."

Max's face grows anxious. "Then move it! We've got to make it to the lighthouse!"

"Sounds about right by me," I tell her.

Only then, just as I'm about to spring down to her, the hackles on the back of my neck shiver, and something turns me back to the *Capricornia* one last time. Just up from the waterline, inside the doorway that leads to the casino, stands Celeste. Etched in charcoal, she's wearing those same cutoff jeans and black T-shirt, but this time, her head's got that nasty gash from her lighthouse jump. Blood stains her forehead. One leg is crooked inside her pants, bent at an impossible angle. Celeste leans away from the busted leg, into the slanted frame, and she fixes me with her eyes. *Looks like you messed up good again, eh, Eli?*

I take a single step toward her, and she seems pleased by this. *You'll never make it, Eli. No point in trying.*

Max yells, "Yo! What's your deal?"

Just stay, Eli! Don't you leave me!

These are the last words my sister ever said to me, when she was dying on the rocks and I told her I was going to get help in her truck.

"Eli!" Max hollers behind me.

I don't take my eyes off Celeste when I answer over my shoulder. "It's my sister," I say. "She's here." Celeste smiles when she hears this, glad to be recognized as real.

"Bullshit," Max yells. "Your head's twisted up in a million ways. You need to get your butt in this boat now! You need to—" I'm sure that Max keeps talking, but her voice fades away. The rope attached to the life raft slips from my grasp. All my world becomes Celeste, begging me, *Stay, stay, stay.*

I don't feel the same fear as strong as I have before. Instead, I feel calm as I approach her. She blinks and smiles at me, and I can see the slick shine of blood on her face, a darker patch along her hair where it's started to crust. It could be that if I reached out to touch her, she'd be solid as a hatchet. But I find now that I don't need to test this theory. It doesn't matter to me if she's real or not.

When she reaches for me with her free hand, the other hanging on the busted doorframe, she doesn't stretch out as if to hug or lean on me. She goes to grab me by the wrist. I step back, and her smile melts to a nasty frown. Whatever she is, this Celeste doesn't mean to embrace me. She means to take hold and drag me down.

Stay, the shade's voice insists. *All that's out there is more screwups.*

"No," I say, slowly shaking my head side to side. "I'm sorry. And I'll love you all the days I got. But you made your choices. Now I need to make mine."

This comes out of me with more conviction than I thought I had, and the spirit Celeste rears back. In the ivory moonlight, I watch the edges of her penciled form start to fade, as if being erased. She looks at me with drowning eyes, and I don't look away. My sister's ghost crumbles to nothing but black ash, and she's gone.

I spin and start running up the tilted deck, drawn by Max's yelling, charging upward, bursting with energy I don't know where from, and when I get to the railing, I don't climb it, I just leap, out into the open air. I see Max in the raft, floating fifty feet away, and beyond her the distant lighthouse. There's an instant that I feel certain I'll just lift away. I feel so light I could take flight.

And it's here, floating through the open air, that I hear Celeste's real voice. It's not the charcoal ghost whispering just in my mind. I hear it in the air around me, and it's clear and true. My sister, the loving one I lost, tells me one last time, "Attaboy."

Chapter Sixteen

MAX SEES ELI RISE OVER THE RAILING OF THE *CAPRICORNIA* wreck, flailing as if he'd been catapulted. His body plummets downward, and he crashes sideways into the rolling waves of the storm-tossed gulf, fifty feet away. She sees the splash and then, after a few tense breaths of nothing, the bright orange life vest appears on the turbulent surface. The choppy waves grow with each undulation, sharper and taller, not only rocking the life raft but also stealing Eli from her view. She grabs one of the boards she'd scavenged moments before and begins to paddle madly, digging at the water. But this lopsided effort only causes the boat to rotate uselessly. A wave lifts the far edge of the life raft, nearly dumping her into the ocean, and she leans back into the middle of the heaving boat.

Through the thickening rain, she catches a glimpse of Eli here and there. He's swinging his arms, struggling to swim, and she cups her hands to her mouth and shouts his name into the wind. As she rides the waves, kneeling in the raft's center, it seems Eli may indeed be getting closer. Whether it's because of his efforts or just the motion of the swirling waters, she can't tell. But soon, he's near enough that she can make out his face, see his one good eye wide in desperation, his gaping mouth sucking for air. A wooden chunk of wreckage slides over a wave's crest and she watches Eli grab for it, only to have it race past him, out of reach. Another wave sloshes over his head, and he lifts an open hand straight up.

Max's eyes swivel around the raft's perimeter until she finds the rope they used as a tether. She snatches it up, reels the full length into a loop, then flings it toward her friend. The wind bats it down, dropping the lasso into the water not ten feet from the raft, nowhere near Eli. Max tries again, and this time the rope simply unfurls.

The current seems to be spinning Eli and the raft around each other, as if they're circling a drain, about twenty feet apart. He's doing some sort of lame doggy-paddle, barely keeping his mouth above the water as far as Max can tell. But it's also clear that his strength is fading, that the life vest can only do so much. Eli is dying before her eyes.

Once again, she reels in the tether rope, keeping a watch on the bobbing orange vest. Only this time when she finds the rope's end, she threads it through her belt, tying off a quick knot. No sooner has she cinched it tight than she's over the side of the raft, diving into the churning waves.

Max feels no panic as she swims in the direction of where she last saw Eli. With each jagged peak, she rises up and slides down, scissoring her legs and swinging her arms. When she can get a clear breath, she hollers, "Eli! Eli, come to my voice!"

She hears a faint cry, the exact word swallowed by the storm, but it gives her a rough location, and she tries to head toward it. It's a strain to fight for every stroke and kick, and Max has no clear sense of whether she's going anywhere or just treading water. But then—incredibly—Eli appears, on his back and motionless, drifting in the swales not too far off. With a burst, she closes that last distance.

Max grips Eli's vest with both hands. She tilts him upright, bringing his face to hers, and he blinks at her and manages to say, "You should've stayed where you were safe."

"Like hell," she tells him. "Now hang on to me and don't let go! Got it?"

She sets his hands on her own life vest, and Eli nods weakly. Then she reaches for the rope around her belt, finds it, and starts to tug. Fist over fist, she makes slow and steady progress through the rolling valley of waves, and she can't tell if she's pulling herself to the raft or pulling the raft to them, but she doesn't care. All that matters is it's growing larger, drawing nearer.

"Eli!" she screams when it's finally within arm's reach. "You need to climb up inside there. Take hold and climb up!"

Max is amazed when he actually does what she says, clawing his way over the rounded inflatable side and collapsing into the raft. She follows, and for a few moments, they lie on their backs, straining for breath. But then Max rolls over and says, "Break time's over. This storm's only getting stronger again. We need to make it to that lighthouse."

Flat on his back, Eli looks exhausted and spent, but she sees a strange smile on his face. He turns onto his belly and gets onto all fours, grinning still. As they gather themselves, Max can't help but ask, "So what happened back there?"

Eli wipes at his face. "Last scene of a long story. One that went on way too long." He gropes for one of the makeshift paddles and lifts his head. "Which way to the lighthouse?"

Max points to the tall white column. The clouds have swallowed the half-moon, so Lucy is just barely visible through the slanting sheets of rain. Eli nods and drapes his chest over one side of the raft. Max takes a position opposite him, and together they start viciously paddling, coaxing the boat toward safety.

With every stroke, Max can't be sure they're doing any good. It's as if they're on a fluid roller coaster, constantly lifting and dipping on the rollicking waves. Though they don't talk, now and then Max spares a look at Eli, every time finding him working that board steady as a machine. She's surprised that he hasn't passed out. Tumbleweeds of low dirty clouds spin overhead as the sky darkens to midnight black.

Maybe it's the waves as much as their efforts that brings them, eventually, into the shadow of the lighthouse. It looms above them, uncaring, as they drift past with no way to stop themselves. And it seems for an instant that they'll miss their chance, simply float inland, but then the raft stops abruptly, even as the waves roll by.

"Get that rope!" Max hears Eli yelling. "Tie us off!"

Max scrambles across the raft's fabric floor and finds Eli leaning over the side, gripping what she realizes is the top of the cyclone fence. She snatches the tether and bends by him, both of them being lifted by the rocking boat but holding steady. After she's anchored them, she says, "Now what?"

Eli hands her the backpack and says, "We abandon ship!"

The twenty feet to the lighthouse looks like a fast-flowing river you wouldn't try to cross, but Eli and Max slip over the side, into the tumultuous sea. "Stay close," Eli yells as they fight toward the tower. The twisting current shoves and tugs them, even tries to draw them down below the waves. They each suck gulps of air and tilt their heads back into their life vests. At one point, Max gets swamped by a swell and feels a hand yank her back to the surface. And then a thick wave gathers them up, sweeps them along, and drives them into the great curved wall of the lighthouse.

"Grab something!" Eli yells.

Max's hands run along the wall, and her eyes scan for some nook or corner. "Nothing to hold," she yells back. Above her, just out of reach, is a window with the glass broken out, a thick iron frame like a cross. "C'mon!" she hears Eli say as he scoots along the wall, hugging it. They work their way around the tower. It takes them a while, battling the cresting waves, but they find themselves again below the window. Max asks, "Where's that damn door?"

"Beneath us," Eli says flatly. "Underwater."

In the raging water, it's a battle to stay in place. "Then we've got to go down," Max yells, saying what she's sure Eli already knows. "We'll dive together."

"Right," Eli answers. "But not with these things on."

Max isn't sure what he means until Eli starts unbuckling his life vest. She watches in shock. The vests are the only things keeping them from drowning, and once they release them, they'll be on their own, at the mercy of the hurricane. "What if we don't find the way in? We'll never get back to the raft." She glances in its direction and sees it, the twenty feet looking like a hundred miles.

Eli tugs his arm through the life jacket, then folds both arms over it. He shrugs. "I figure at that point we pucker up and kiss our butts good-bye."

"This is nuts," she says as she passes the backpack to Eli and goes about removing her own life jacket. When she's finished, she retrieves the backpack, and then the two of them bob on the surface, holding hands, each with the other arm around a bunched-up vest.

"Get a deep breath," Eli says, and together, they let go of the vests and descend.

Under the water, the sound of the storm is muted. Everything is darkness and a muffled, distant roar. Max kicks down, vaguely aware of Eli at her side, and she stretches in the inky black, feeling the wall's rock hard certainty with an open palm. It feels good to give in to the weight of the urn, to let it drag her deeper still. With effort, she flips head down, fluttering feet now up above. Her eyes blink in the darkness, but nothing can be seen.

And then her fingers find a break in the wall's constant shape, an edge, a corner below. She reaches out for Eli, locates a handful of cloth, and tugs, urging him downward. Using the top of the open entryway, she pulls herself deeper, flipping upside down through the threshold that once housed the door, and then quickly rising up, lifting with the last of the air in her lungs, bursting to the surface inside the lighthouse.

She swings her arms in the pitch black, bangs into stairs, and crawls out of the circular pool of water. It's surprisingly calm, just sloshing gently, and Max waits in the stillness. She thinks, *C'mon, Eli. Don't you*—but then he too erupts from the surface, gasping for new breath. "Here!" she says, reaching out for him and pulling him to her on the curving stairs.

"We made it!" he yells. In response, the wind shrieks through the broken window above them and a wave bashes the outside wall, hard enough that they can feel the building shudder.

Eli sits up. "We need to climb. Let's get away from this water."

Rather than stand on weary legs, the two of them crawl on their hands and knees, slowly ascending the nautilus stairway curving along the inner wall of the lighthouse. They pause at the windows, more for a break than a chance to take in the dark view. When they do look out, all they can make out is black and gray mixing, water and wind swirling together.

Eventually, Eli stops. Max hears him knock on something above them, and he says, "Can't go no farther. The water'll never get this high. We're safe, so long as Lucy don't crumble."

"That's a positive thought," she says back. Like a blind man, Max pats at the backpack, feeling with her fingers to find the zipper and tug it open. She reaches inside to locate a long, thin tube. She tears open the wrapper and shakes the glow stick, bringing a welcome yellow-green shine into the chamber. It's not much but enough that they can see the metal trapdoor above them, and they can make out each other's faces.

Eli, battered and bruised, still manages a grin and says, "Aren't you mighty resourceful? We'll make a Southern girl out of you yet."

Max is positioned a few steps below Eli, sitting between his bent knees on the narrow stairs. She sees something on the wall by his face, at the edge of the glow, and she turns and works her way up, bringing her head over his chest. Extending her arm, she illuminates the wall and reads the words scrawled there: "Heather Loves Blake!" After a moment, she declares, "Those two lovebirds sure are fond of graffiti."

Without thinking, she rests her face on Eli's chest, just below his chin. He drapes an arm over her shoulder, sliding it inside the backpack's strap, and she's not sure but she thinks she feels him pull her into him a bit. "What would you write?" Eli asks. "Assuming you had the means?"

She thinks for a minute, and she can feel his chest rising and falling softly. "I can't think of anything good. What about you?"

He's quiet for a time, then says, "Eli and Max. Damn hard to kill."

Max laughs and says, "I like it. It does seem like we've had nine lives lately."

"We only have the one," Eli says. "Just using it good."

She picks up her head to look at him, and his eyes catch on hers. They draw each other closer, and she eases her mouth up to meet Eli's. Their lips press together softly at first, hesitant. But then they kiss without reserve, feeling the thrill of the life they have left.

When Max lifts a hand to caress Eli's cheek, she drops the glow stick, and they break their kiss. Together they watch it, like a falling star, plummeting down the lighthouse's interior, streaking light behind it. Neither one sees it hit bottom. It's just gone.

"Your fault for distracting me," Max says.

Eli laughs a little. "I thought you were distracting me."

She begins to shuffle for the backpack and says, "Hang on. I got one more."

"We should save it," Eli suggests. He settles one hand along the nape of her neck and guides her head back to his chest, which makes for her a fine enough pillow. "We may need the light later. No way of knowing what's ahead."

She slides her hands under his arms, reaching up to cup his shoulders. And he crosses his wrists across her back, hugging her into him.. Inside this embrace, she feels safe in a way that's hard to name. They are so totally alone here in this dark womb yet so totally together, reliant on each other. She's certain that Eli feels the same way. Before long, Max hears his breath shifting and wonders if he might not pass out. Still, she's sure that for as long as the storm rages, they will cling to each other with all the strength they possess.

Time passes oddly for Max. With no watch and no light, she can't tell as the minutes come and go and the hours bleed together in darkness. The hurricane winds whip around the lighthouse, and any lulls are filled with the crescendo of crashing waves. It becomes a strange sound track as she slides in and out of consciousness, flashes of memory striking up in her mind: the morning her mother was gone, and all day her dad drank whiskey from a coffee mug. The drive south to Louisiana, her navigating by map while he steered, and all those bad gas station meals. Angie telling her she looked pretty as she stood before a dressing room mirror. Her father's face in the hospital, his cracked lips and his rattling breath. And when she was leaving Wayne Osteopathic that last time, in the hallway, her eyes had settled on Angie's bulging belly. Angie saw this, reached for Max's wrist, and guided her hand toward her stomach, saying, "The baby's kicking. You want to feel?" But Max had recoiled, snapped her hand back, and marched away.

All these things and other memories sit heavy on Max's mind, haunting her in and out of a fevered sleep. She doesn't notice the winds gradually fading, the rains abating, the sea calming itself. It's Eli, awake once more, who stirs and says, "Hey. You hear that?"

Startled, she lifts her face from his chest, wipes her teary cheeks, and says, "Hear what?"

In response, Eli shifts his weight, then slides out from under Max. A few moments later, dim light spills into the chamber as he raises the rusty metal door above them. It squeaks on cranky hinges, then clangs down hard, and they climb up into the crow's nest, where they first met just the day before.

It's like a movie, Max thinks. One of those apocalyptic flicks where the world meets its doom. The gulf spreads endlessly all around them, as if they're in the middle of a vast ocean, like they're the last souls left on earth. Strewn along the surface is unrecognizable wreckage—splintered wood, debris, shattered tree branches, flotillas of garbage. Max wonders how much is from the casino boat, how much the drifting remains of Eli's destroyed hometown. She scans the ocean for the oil rigs and finds the horizon wiped clean.

Right below them, the orange life raft floats peacefully, still tied to the fence, waiting like a loyal dog. The early morning sky is a light gray dome, with a few wispy white clouds threading along silently. Max is struck by a strange absence. "There's no birds," she says.

Eli doesn't respond. He just grips a railing and stares east toward town.

She steps up behind him and sets one hand on his shoulder, just so he knows she's there. Finally, he says, "My home," and she can tell he's not just talking about the house where he grew up, which no doubt is gone, but the entire community.

Unsure of what else to offer, she says, "I'm sorry."

Eli shrugs and turns to answer. "You got a habit of apologizing when you didn't do anything wrong. You know?" They tilt toward each other and hug, and it feels good having his arms around her and good to squeeze him back. He feels solid and steady. When he breaks the embrace, Max thinks they might kiss again, but instead, Eli steps away from her. She watches him descend through the trapdoor. He returns holding the backpack, and he sets it on the stumpy foundation that used to hold the beacon light. Eli reaches through the zippered opening and pulls free her father's urn. He offers it to her and says, "We got some serious rowing ahead of us. I figure it's about time you did what you set out to do."

She extends both hands and accepts the boxy weight. The urn is cold and heavier than she'd remembered. She grips the top and with effort pries up the stubborn lid. There's a small pop of air. When she looks inside, she finds a simple plastic bag, tied with a white piece of lace. She tugs the bow to undo the knot. The contents of the bag look like fine gray sand, and Max imagines what it would feel like to pinch this dust between her fingertips.

This is the scene she'd envisioned on the long trip south, through Baltimore, Washington, Atlanta, Mobile, New Orleans. All that way, she'd driven without music, keeping silent and picturing the handfuls of ash she'd toss into the clear air, the swirling dust that was all that remained of her father. It would drift from her fingertips and scatter into nothingness. How good it would feel, she'd convinced herself, to see him released and be free of how she'd wronged him. How sweet it would be, to simply let go.

But now, as she stares down into the bag, other images crowd her mind. Angie is alone in the empty house, one hand resting on her belly, sitting at the kitchen table, praying for the phone to ring. Surely the search for her wild stepdaughter will turn up something. Surely her husband's last remains will be recovered.

Max shoves the lid back on, resealing the urn. "I'm good to go," she tells Eli. Maybe after she gets back to Jersey and comes clean with Angie, on the far side of some long talks and hard apologies, they will return to this place. Or maybe they'll go back to Mr. Clayborne and bring her dad to that cemetery by Angie's church. But they'll decide together how best to honor her father. This, Max feels in her heart, is what a good daughter would do.

Eli smiles and nods, and Max thinks somehow he understands. She finds herself thinking of the funeral home, the hot office of that sweaty man, and the weird framed expression on his wall. She's trying to recall the peculiar words when Eli pats the concrete stump. "Looks like we'll have to put our restoration project on hold. With all the storm damage, nobody's gonna want to put money into an old lighthouse."

They wander back to the railing and survey the distant damage. She says, "You think they'll be able to salvage anything from town?"

Eli shakes his head. "For the most part, I suspect there'll be nothing left but the foundations. The Shacks has got more new construction in its future than repair work. Sometimes it's better to just demolish the remains of what was and start fresh."

Max nods. She learned from her dad: Sometimes a property can only suffer so much damage and there's no point in trying to restore it. The best bet is to tear it down and start from scratch. Max feels like she's been torn down herself, and she likes this notion of a new beginning. She asks Eli, "You think I'll make a good big sister?"

He says, "Better than most."

It looks like he's about to add something more when his eyes catch on something above them. His head turns, and Max tracks his gaze. High above them, a single bird soars over the disaster. Max can't tell if it's one of those herons or just a seagull, but it's winging its way east, back toward the main part of the island. As Max watches it fly, something steals her attention in the waters below.

Cutting through the junk and crap, a lone Jet Ski releases a high whine into the silence. It navigates the floating debris with sharp, sweeping curves, leaving a V in its wake. Max says, "Does the Coast Guard have boats like that?"

Eli grins and says, "This here's gonna be way better than the Coast Guard. Come on."

By the time they reach the windowless iron frame near the water, Sweeney has pulled up and is idling below the opening. He doesn't look at all surprised to come across them like this, and Max notices a bloom of blood on the field bandage encircling his left bicep. A huge set of binoculars hangs from his neck. He raises his right arm in greeting. "Made my way to the Chains looking for you two. Then saw the lighthouse and figured what the hell. Stranger things have happened." His gaze falls on the bright raft. "Where'd you pull that from?"

"Long story," Eli says. "How's our town?"

Sweeney glances over his shoulder, as if checking. "Not much more than a memory. Least for now."

And Max hears it again, the promise of rebuilding. She asks, "What about Charity and the kids?"

Sweeney beams. "High and dry. Kind of rattled by the 'cane, but they were coming around when I left on patrol. That little one, Sabine? Safe to say something's a bit off about that child, yeah?"

Eli and Max exchange looks. She says, "Something's a bit off about everybody down here."

Careful to avoid the hunks of floating rubble, Eli and Max jump into the water and swim to the swamped raft. Because of all the rain and sea wash, they need to dump it sideways. Next they find the knot at the fence, so waterlogged and tight they just cut the rope with Sweeney's knife. He attaches the free end to his Jet Ski and, though the engine complains at the weight, he begins to tow them slowly in the direction he came.

Eli and Max lean back into the stern of the raft, side by side. Above them the sky gradually regains a healthy glow. Color is returning to the world. As they motor toward town, the debris scattered on the surface becomes thicker: roofing tiles, huge chunks of soggy drywall, the top half of a trailer home, a single red sneaker, a bare mattress, the bloated belly of some poor animal's carcass. Max cranes her head for a final glance at the lighthouse, diminishing in size as they move farther away. As it shrinks, she asks Eli, "Aren't you going to give it one last look?"

But Eli keeps his face fixed forward. "I'm not especially concerned with what's behind me just now. I've got my mind set somewhere up ahead."

Max turns to the water tower rising in the distance. She imagines the iron bridge beneath it and the road that will lead back to the life she fled. With one hand, Max holds the urn close, but with the other, she reaches for Eli, folding her fingers around his. Like this, they watch a white heron float above them. Somehow it too survived the storm, and it pulses now on unsteady wings, leading the way.

ACKNOWLEDGMENTS

I am grateful to my agent, Sara Crowe, for her faith in my writing. As for Cheryl Klein, if editors were graded like hurricanes for their power, she'd be a Category 6.

ABOUT THE AUTHOR

Neil Connelly is the author of five novels, including *St. Michael's Scales*, which *Kirkus* described as a "richly layered, thought-provoking novel of how one boy learns to make weight," and *The Miracle Stealer*, which *Booklist* called "realistic, gutsy— and yet movingly spiritual" in a starred review. Neil weathered five hurricanes in Lake Charles, Louisiana, in the course of seventeen years. He now lives with his wife and two sons in the calmer climes of central Pennsylvania, where he teaches creative writing at Shippensburg University. You can find him on the web at www.neilconnelly.com.

This book was edited by Cheryl Klein and designed by Mary Claire Cruz. The text was set in Adobe Caslon Pro. The book was printed and bound at R.R. Donnelly in Crawfordsville, Indiana. The manufacturing was supervised by Angelique Browne.